DOUBLE DUTCH

Some 411 on 911

Brookshire G. IV

Renewing Your Mind Ink
A division of
Renewing Your Mind Foundation, Inc
315 Dartmouth Drive
Unit 535
Marshalls Creek, PA 18335

ISBN-13: 978-1-58441-007-2
Library of Congress Control Number: 2024901826

This book is offered in the historical/fiction genre, with that said it's written to only entertain. My writing style is not traditional. There's some poetry infused in the narrative. The only truth in this story is the word of God. I wouldn't be the man I say l am if I didn't mention some scripture, that is out of context. [Just try to enjoy.]

I'm a child of God, an Air Force veteran, a son, a husband, and a father. I say this because someone could read this story and feel that I don't have respect for first responders. The event that happened on 9-11-2001 was a bad situation to be in and then die. I must mention those who survived. They have increasing health problems, some unto death even today. I take my hat off, bow my head, and put my hand over my heart to express my condolences.

Regarding the character named Me, I find it necessary to remind you that this book is a work of fiction. I, the author, am not him. This narrative is simply moving toward the power that is perceived by the main players of having money. [Just try to enjoy.] You may read this tall tale and decide I've disrespected the hero who just came to work that day only to serve. You could then think I've removed the first responders from the seat of honor. I have not. It's only in this imaginary remix of love lost, revenge, and catastrophe that a hero dies for nothing more than a robbery. [Just try to enjoy] Now that I have that off my chest, I can do and be better. I can be and do better.Read this book with a raised eyebrow. This dream may seem to make light of the 911 event. I say all of us have PTSD—America in the aftermath. We're thinking, *What the hell is happening? Who is responsible for this? Why, on the 9th month and the 11th day, is a whole zip code trying to make a 911 call? Who is the person speaking? Who is the person spoken to?* All over the United States, looking and listening for answers.

The powers that be had the media tell us some things. Its words calmed some people down and it fired some people up. Our leaders pointed a finger. "Never Forget" was the battle cry as we came together and charged forward. We found no mass destruction-type weapons when we got there. Our leaders pointed a different finger somewhere else and started a war lasting twenty years. Now we come together yearly to remember. The difference today is after the memorial services, we go back to our corners of left, right, Black, White, and the people who have and the people who don't have enough. 911 put a pause on many of us and put an end to the lives of three hundred forty-three firefighters, including the thousands of other people who left home for work that day, never to return. I stand and salute those people. The story reflects the thinking of people who, for reasons of their own, lose their grip on sound judgement. The characters think revenge and a few billion dollars for each of them is the cure, in a world where there is much lack, it seems. Controversy and conspiracy are an interesting mix these days. Just try to enjoy.

Controversy.

Conspiracy.

Fake news.

On this elevator ride, it's just another day you have taken for granted…until it isn't. To presume that the ride up to your office on this day will be as smooth as the ride down yesterday is a grossly underestimated assumption. You would be one of thousands going to work today that will feel extreme heat. You will see no way to escape the fire. Many will consider something they may not have thought about since the first day on the job—and that is the magnificent view from this high up.

"Do I jump?"

Those who make it to the stairs run as fast as they can. Imagine running out of shoes and leaving them behind. The concrete cloud of dust is upon you and your co-workers, breathing in the debris. You survive, but people die months later. Your shortness of breath is evidence of being there on that fateful day, and you know that your life will never be the same.

Americans have noticed the world's landscape has changed. We have less freedom and more surveillance than ever. We have a war that has never really ended as of today. A lot of lives fade to black but are never forgotten.

The book *Double Dutch* is a tale of the deception in an event just short of conspiracy. It feeds the flames of all involved, where acts of revenge and greed rule the day as we find some 411 on 911.

CHAPTER 1

It is one bright day in the middle of the night.
Three dead boys got up to fight.
One pulled out a gun, and someone was stabbed.
Another pulls out a knife, and someone gets shot.
An old deaf man heard the noise.
And he prayed the Word over the three dead boys.
The boys were living a lie; now they know the Truth.
If you don't believe this lie can be taught as true.
Ask the blind man, he can see, too.

I have thoughts that float in and then out of my mind; who's to say? I say.

One night after work, I head out to a poetry club where the spoken word reigns supreme, joining some of my friends. It's not unlike other Friday nights, though not every Friday is the same; sometimes we gather in the parking lot to discuss work, life, world issues, and more. This time, things are different. I don't remember who first told us about this spot, but there we were.

Among us are Finelle, Brain, Jay, Cleo, Dave, Nick, Berry, Peanut, Elvis, Pier, Franz, Russo, Scott, Derrick, Drew, Spot, Jimmy, Chris, Ivory, Will, Phillip, Charles, Frank, Garland, and others. Most tables accommodate three or four people.

A thin cloth obscures the person on stage. I assume there's a light behind him because all I can see is his shadow on the thin fabric. Judging by the voice, I guess it's a man. He's holding a guitar, just grasping it for now. The announcer steps onto the stage and looks around at the audience.

"Welcome to the people and the poets to the club Double Dutch.
In this place, everyone has paid a price.
It's Friday night and we have the stage that gives sight to the looker.
Give us a piece of your mind and we'll eat it right here.
Whether you be preaching
Or it smells like teaching you stepped in from the world streets.
We will record the moment
When fame gives recognition to courage,
Courage over fear
Double Dutch archives will have proof
You be living.
Now, without further delay, I give you Open Mic."

It sounds like improvisation, off-the-cuff. I shrug, thinking, *I can do that.* You know, if I wore the same hat and stood behind a very thin, red veil, one might mistake me for him. Let's hear what he has to say. We sit, we drink, and we eat.

"*Middle Class*

And what about? What do you do to fill the hole with?

The gap between now and upper or the slippery slope to lower.

Reality says buy one of these. But you have one.

Buy another one, faster maybe another color, in case they stop making that model.

You're still trying to fill the hole. You read.

The knowledge makes you sad.

You read that we're not slaves, but you find you're not free either.

After the weekend off or vacation now over and its back to work.

You put your riches in the hole, and you enjoy all you can do.

Now you're chained to the money, and you can't do without it.

Someone leads you to Living Water and the Bread of Life.

You find it feels the whole world. Made free you are.

You don't see your ghetto as it is, but as it should be.

You no longer have an excuse, but you still have issues.

You have too much income to get help benefits, but make too little to change the outcome.

I'm just saying.

You are shown down the street to a second heaven. The word on the corner is that this is the devil's prison.

In this realm, the armies fight a losing battle for your soul against the angels of God. At times

delaying the message.

Say it isn't so. What happened?

Daniel is ten, and well….

You will receive the message.

You see people you thought you knew doing things and saying things contrary to their outward character.

Perplexed to see the war fought without guns and knives, but words that cut deep. Deceit is the weapon of choice with the illusion of happiness.

The skin wanting to feel all Jezebel has to offer.

The eyes want to see as much of Jezebel as it can see and it's never enough.

You can't have enough here, always wanting more and bigger.

You feel down in your spirit,

Not your position.

A spirit wants to worship from that you are.

Please Him. The God in the Good Book.

Love is His way, written on scrolls and copied off rocks.

Tell you He is. Teach your spirit and live each day in it.

The body is dead but will remember. The spirit rules the member.

Power over the body. I am Open Mic. More Peace."

Anyway, it's almost time for me to leave. I've had a couple of drinks, so I think I'll have one more for the road.

I go to the bar for a shot of Johnnie Walker Black on the Rocks, a drink with ice for those who've never ordered a drink from a bar. I stand there, waiting to order, and I notice a couple having what seems like a heated discussion. Out of nowhere, the guy smacks the girl in the face. Her reaction isn't surprising. She grabs her face and her purse, then runs out of the club crying. I watch her retreating back and think, *Can't we just have a good time?*

I guess that's life sometimes. Not everyone is having a good time. With a deep breath, I shake my head and decide to have a glass of water instead. I've had enough of this night. I turn away from the bar and head back to my seat. As I'm turning, I look the guy directly in his eyes. Now I'm feeling conflicted about the whole situation. I'm trying not to judge. I don't know why he hit her. My upbringing taught me to never hit a lady unless it's self-defense.

The guy tilts his head and looks at me enigmatically. "Well, what are you looking at?"

"Nothing." I walk past him.

"That's what I thought." In all his smugness, my insult goes right over his head.

By now, I'm back at the table. Cleo, Jay, and Berry are gone. I guess they went for drinks to another part of the club. As I turn to sit down, Cleo is right behind me.

"Did you see what happened at the bar?"

He nods. "I try to stay out of grown folks' business now. The last time I tried to break up a fight at a little house party,

I got cut in the face along one of my sideburns. The mark is gone, but the hair will not grow in that line."

We sit down and listen to the rest of what Open Mic is talking about—something about having too much money and not enough at the same time.

Cleo, who favors Ice Cube, the rapper, transferred from another ABX station during the merger. We punch the clock at a parcel pickup and delivery company, very much like UPS or FedEx. This company has been in business for sixty-three years and has been losing money for a few years while trying to compete in the Bush II economy. You can add to that mix some bad management, plus every nine or eleven drivers are trying to stick it to the company for a few dollars as payback for any reason, from being shortened in their pay on their last check, to unfair, unwarranted disciplinary actions. The reasons seem endless, including issues like trucks with no air-conditioning, causing drivers to delay pickups and deliveries to grab a cold drink of water, tea, soda, or my favorite, iced coffee.

On a one hundred and one-degree day, we get some relief when it drops to eighty degrees at night. The company is Airborne Express or ABX on the stock exchange page reader. In the face of the Bush II economic climate, ABX was in the act of combining stations to cover customers with less overhead.

During that same time, ABX began entertaining buyout offers from other companies like UPS, FedEx, and DHL, a company located in Germany. It sits under the umbrella of Deutsche Bank. They are said to rival or surpass the US Postal service while serving all of Europe. It's striking to see a DHL station that is currently trying to acquire us, right across the street from our two merging ABX stations.

Funny story. Cleo calls the house one day. My wife answers the phone.

Cleo says, "Hello, can I speak to my man?"

My wife replies, "That's *my* man." Yes, she went there.

At the time, I didn't know who was on the phone. I glance at her, wondering, *Who is she talking to?*

She looks at me and hands me the phone. "Here, it's Cleo."

Now I'm laughing, but she's not.

Cleo asks me, "What was that all about?"

I tell him it wasn't his problem; she was just making sure he knew I was her man, not his.

Cleo's voice changes. "What!" I explain it's a long story related to things she went through in her first marriage. Cleo says, "Y'all trippin'."

With a smirk, I think, *That's life in the big city.*

Most of the guys I hang out with play basketball on the weekends and then we cool down with some beers. Some even bring their wives and kids to watch, which is what Jay, Berry, Cleo, and I have in common.

On the weekend, Cleo is a no-show, so I ask, "Hey, Cleo, what happened to you over the weekend? Why didn't you show up to play ball?"

"Man, I hurt my foot playing basketball last week. It got worse, so I won't be playing much for a while."

You learn a lot about folks when you're drinking and talking. All of us have something in common besides working together. Cleo has one of those lives that looks most like mine. I realize while talking that we've walked over some of the same paths. Like me, he's ex-military, also Air Force, and has been married once. He has a grown daughter, and I have a son somewhere in California. Neither of us likes to be disrespected, but who does? He has an opinion about most subjects, right or wrong, as most people do after a few drinks. Like most of us, he feels his situation could be better, but it's cool because it could be worse. He cuts hair as a side hustle. I used to own a hair salon. He seems to be good people coming from good God-fearing parents, but as I heard my nephew say, "I know you, but I don't know you."

Berry is married, has children, and is about six-foot-five. Jay, on the other hand, is not married and plays guard. He is also the union shop steward and is generally well-liked among us.

Some finger popping and bongo playing, and then the stage fades to black. It's another break in the show, and I've had enough of this night. Cleo decides he's heading out the door, too.

As we make our way toward the exit, the heavy bass thumping in the club dims behind us. Just as we reach the door, it swings open, and four police officers stroll inside.

Cleo leans over to me, his voice low with curiosity. "What's happening?"

I shrug, scanning the officers as they move through the crowd toward the bar. The doorman, a burly figure with a no-nonsense expression, catches our eye.

Cleo gestures toward the commotion. "Hey, what's going on in there?"

The doorman looks around cautiously before leaning in, his voice barely audible over the music. "There's been an incident in the men's restroom. A man's been found dead."

I exhale sharply. "Damn, really?"

Cleo nods grimly. "Should we stay and find out more?"

Before we can decide, more police cars pull up outside, lights flashing silently in the night. An officer steps out and motions for the crowd to disperse. "Everyone, please return inside the club. We're investigating a serious matter."

Reluctantly, we comply, filing back through the entrance. The air feels heavy with tension, conversations hushed, and eyes darting nervously around.

"Can I ask you a few questions?" an officer asks.

I exchange a glance with Cleo, tension knotting in my stomach. "Sure, officer. What do you need to know?"

"Did you see anything unusual tonight?"

Cleo shakes his head, his voice steady. "No, nothing out of the ordinary."

"And did they scan your driver's license when you entered?"

I nod, looking at Cleo, who also nods. "Yes, they did."

"All right. Thank you for your cooperation."

As the officer moves away, I can't shake the feeling that things could have been very different if our answers had been reversed.

I don't know either person involved. I guess he smacked the wrong girl.

CHAPTER 2

It is a good day and a normal drive home with no traffic. My sixty-five-mile commute on Mondays includes a gas fill-up, as Mondays and Thursdays are six cents off per gallon. I use premium fuel for the 8-cylinder engine made by Bentley. While I don't drive a Bentley, they make the engine in my Volkswagen. Most people don't believe me, so I avoid mentioning it to dodge skeptical looks. It only comes up when discussing cars. When I'm parked next to a Lexus or BMW, I point out that a luxury vehicle leader makes my car's engine. Despite this, I paid exactly what the car was worth, and I could have bought a Mercedes Benz E320 for that kind of money. I don't quite fit in the E-Class Benz, so I chose comfort over a bit more style. The car uses super gasoline, so I fill up on discount days at BP gas stations, saving about one hundred three dollars a year with an 18-gallon purchase. Every bit helps.

I arrive home and set down the keys and an empty water bottle, then take off with my shoes and clothes, have a quick shower, and get into bed. I skip TV, drinks to help me sleep, and a midnight snack. All I can think about is last Friday, and the constant driving has made me tired. It feels like I've been working two jobs all week. After some tossing and turning, the sandman arrives. I wonder, *Who started calling sleep the Sandman?* THIS IS MY DAILY ROUTINE. A change in the pattern would include all the things I skipped tonight: a little TV, especially if there's an NBA game in the fourth quarter from the West Coast, snacks to go with that, and if I had coffee after 8:00 p.m., maybe a shot of something to help me sleep soundly through the night.

I call my wife to let her know I'll be a little late and to not worry. "If you need me, call the club and have me paged. I might not hear my cell."

I run through the club, opening doors, unsure if the people behind me are with me or after me. Some are following through the doors I open. I see many doors open and I run past several of them, trying to stay ahead of the people behind me. I go through a door and suddenly, I'm outside, in my car—a sleek black 1999 Grand Prix. Without hesitation, I speed off, paying the toll as I head up the mountain.

Once inside the house, the dogs are loose, with free rein. My wife lets them out when she fears noises she can't explain. Usually, we put the dogs away at night in their space near the back basement door. After checking all the windows and doors, and everything seems in order, I let the dogs outside for a perimeter check. They find nothing that keeps them from running back inside when I call them.

I go back upstairs and off with the shoes, wash my face, get out of the clothes, and get in bed. I'm guessing it is 3:00 a.m. or so, but I am too tired to shower or check the time, as I usually do to see how much time I have to sleep.

It feels like my eyes are closed for a minute or two before the dogs are barking, and the baby's calling, "Mommy, Mommy, Mommy, Daddy, Mommy," and she's crying because no one is in her room yet. It's 6:00 a.m., and I slow the wife down long enough to talk to her about Friday night.

"I talked to Cleo when I got to work yesterday. He said we didn't go out Friday after work."

"Did you? Are you sure?"

"It seems like I remember seeing a poet; his stage name was Open Mic. He did his show behind a thin, almost see-through red cloth with lights behind him, creating a shadow effect on the cloth. He sat on a stool, holding a guitar that he had never played. We all had drinks like it was some kind of celebration. I remember paying the toll, and the next thing I knew, I was in front of the house. Oh, and did I mention a man was killed and found in the men's restroom? His right hand was cut up pretty badly."

"No, this is news to me, and news I'd rather not hear at the start of my day, or any time, for that matter. See you tomorrow."

I can't believe what's happening—I'm having problems with my memory and reality. I guess I'll start journaling the events of my life and comment on the effects of said events.

I always had some kind of notepad for as long as I can remember. My plan is to make new entries in a bit more detail. With everything happening on in my life, the situation weighs heavily on me—my children, my life, the impact of race issues and its effect on the war, elections, and the list could go on.

My body hurts a lot—my shoulders, my neck, and my lower back are all injured. I experience daily pain and only take pills on heavy workdays, such as around Christmas.

I try not to take pain pills to manage it, and I normally do not take sleeping pills all day or night. I have a drink of something eighty-proof to bring me down from a late cup of coffee or prevent me from tossing and turning through the night because of my aching feet. One shot, and two birds down without side effects compared to pain pills and sleep aids. I know it's wrong. Some may say, "Just say no," but it's always easy not to feel someone's pain when not in their shoes. I don't take for granted that I'm not on medication constantly.

I imagine starting the day as usual until arriving at work. I see a private vehicle parked inside the station. A handicapped office agent owns the car. Today, like other days, the company parks vans in handicapped spaces and ignores the complaints from the agents. On this day, an agent has had enough. She pulls her car into the station and parks it.

It isn't long before the station manager gets wind of it. He comes out onto the dock to find the car is impeding the afternoon drivers who are preparing for their shifts. No one is telling who the car belongs to, and everyone is having a good laugh. The other drivers don't care either way, mainly because the car isn't in their way.

Without knowing the car's owner, the station manager has to call the tow truck. He calls from his office, passing by the agent who owns the car.

As he hangs up the phone, she tells him, "That's my car."

"Move it."

"No."

"Your car is parked in a prohibited area."

"And so are the company vans outside?"

"What are you talking about?"

"You allow your drivers to park in the only two handicap spaces in the lot. I've asked you to address the matter via e-mail and letters, so I have proof of this correspondence, and of using the proper channels. Now I figure, what's good for the goose is good for the gander. I parked inside. It's better for me anyway, less distance to walk."

She's giving this speech to the boss, a full house of office agents, and all the second-shift drivers, officially interrupting work. Drivers outside the office can see through the dispatch window into the office area; heads and necks are moving, and hands and arms emphasize the sound we can't hear. Now, the tow truck is pulling into the dock, its lights flashing. The boss and agent see through the window and come out to meet the tow truck driver.

The tow truck driver asks, "Which one do I hook up to?"

"The car parked over there."

"Don't touch my car!"

"Then move it!"

"Move it where? All the handicapped spaces have vans in them."

As the tow truck driver starts doing his job, the manager is just standing with arms folded.

The agent has all the attitude. "Let me get this straight. You are going to tow my car instead of moving a van?"

There is no reply from the boss. I guess the agent has seen enough. She takes out her cell phone, calls 911, and reports that someone is stealing her car. She gives the address and hangs up.

Before the tow truck can leave the station, the police arrive with disco lights and sirens. Now no one can leave, including the loaded vans that are ready to start the next shift. Everyone is waiting to see what happens next. The police get both sides of the story, compare notes, and issue citations to the station manager—a one-thousand-dollar fine for each space. Adding insult to injury, he has to unhook the car and still pay for the tow truck call.

Not much time passes, maybe a few days, before the officer's report reveals city code volitions to inspectors.

Considering the number of people working, they decide to add more handicapped spaces in the parking lot. The company has thirty days to paint the new handicap spaces.

After all the commotion, everyone is behind schedule. On top of that, we have a new client to pick up and process. I'm looking at a ten or eleven-hour workday with no lunch; I'll have to eat while I drive, late at night, and have coffee after 8:00 p.m. I knew this from the start. I began pickups at 3:30 p.m. By 6:00 p.m. I pick up one hundred medium-sized boxes, and by 7:30 p.m., I fill up the van and can't take more freight. A driver must meet me on the road on his way back to the station. This delivery driver has been at it since 7:30 a.m. and has a bittersweet attitude. Remember, it's time and a half for any hours worked after 8 hours inside one day. He may get done by 9:30 p.m. tonight.

Most of the day drivers have been around for some time, and their overtime pay rate is around thirty-five dollars an hour. I am back in my empty van when I get the call, letting me know it's okay to work through lunch. Dispatch could have told me to go on to lunch, but it would have caused all kinds of problems, from missed pickup to me leaving work late. I expected the call because I often work through lunch. My overtime rate is twenty-seven dollars an hour, and today I'll work more than one hour over my regular eight hours. I get a Wendy's spicy chicken sandwich, fries, and Mountain Dew.

I've already moved eight hundred pounds of parcel; my back and shoulders are screaming, *Are you taking pain pills tonight?* My answer has been *yes* for some time, so down goes a pill. I still have until 9:15 p.m. to pick up packages and then back to the station by 9:30. My normal day is over at 10:30, but tonight we have to work until midnight to process packages in time for the airport. I head back to the station and stop for coffee. I have a full van again and I have driven one hundred twelve miles. I still have a sixty-five-mile drive home. I guess that explains the Mountain Dew and coffee cocktail. I'm not saying it's okay; I'd rather be awake at home late than half asleep on the road.

I make it home another night safely—thank God. I don't take it for granted that I'll make it. I see brake lights and headlights backed up for miles all the time, like tonight on the eastbound side. It doesn't hold me up this time, but I hate that it has become a routine sight. The reds, oranges, and whites, along with the blue sparks from what looks like a barn fire, set against a forest-black backdrop with the tops of evergreen trees edging the clear night sky and stars, make a beautiful scene. Except you know it's not a barn fire. It's a car fire, and as you move closer, you see and smell the black smoke, even against the dark. I hope no one is inside the car. Then I feel relieved that it's not me involved in the accident or stuck in the traffic jam that stretches as far as I can see, waiting to get around it. I pray for increased strength for everyone involved and that they know Christ Jesus, as the real tragedy would be dying without Him as your Savior.

I'm home now, and before I can think of anything else, I down a shot of Wild Turkey. I'm beat, and then I remember the pain pills I took about five or six hours ago. It's not good for anyone to do this, so it's another reason to pray—especially for the times when I'm not thinking straight. I take a shower, then head to bed. It's around 3:00 a.m. when I fall asleep, thinking about the ten more years before early retirement: five hundred twenty weeks, twenty-six hundred days (not counting Saturdays), and hopefully, not many more days like this one.

After a long week, it's Friday night. Some of the guys and I are in the parking lot, talking about the crazy week over some Cokes and brown juice. It's a cool night with music playing, and Cleo manages to lock his keys in the car after lighting a cigarette with a car lighter. Now everyone is looking for hangers to try to break into the car. From my experience, I know that's going to be hard on a Toyota. Some of the others are drawing straws to see who's going to take him home for his extra set of keys. Amid all this, I find a hanger and walk over to his car. I pull the door handle right before trying to push the hanger down into the window near the lock. I never actually get to use the hanger because the door opens when I pull the handle.

"Cleo, I thought you said the doors were locked?"

"It was. You see the key in the starter."

"Okay, if you say so."

The others don't see what I do; they're still talking about who's taking Cleo home for his keys. Those who are looking are on the other side of the car and just figure I'm good with a hanger. I hear comments like, "That's the last time I leave valuables in the car around you." Cleo sees the whole thing and knows I didn't use a hanger; he knows his doors are all locked. His lack of response to me suggests that he is either unsurprised or skilled at maintaining a poker face.

The cops do a drive-by, and we decide to finish up at the club. I call my wife from the parking lot and tell her I'm at Double Dutch with some of the guys, then I'll be on my way home. We go in and see the man behind the cloth is sitting with a guitar he doesn't play. We find seats and order snacks—chicken fingers and fries for me. Open Mic is on the stage.

"Joy and hopelessness, defeated, on an endless rope of hope, help.
I stand firm with a good grip on the situation's solution.
It is impossible to avoid a certain outcome.
An objective stands on optimistic viewpoints.
Subjectively, now let's analyze that.
I step on.
I try to see life from where
I'm standing and hope to learn something forward from what I'm seeing.
A pain I know to be true.

*The direction is upward, the path straight and yet leaving me
with less strength.*

Only my being still beating and where am I?

Being too weak to move, I make right the wrong thing.

Far too sleepy to be deep in thought, I'm far below that.

This is the sticky film left behind from the day.

I checked the time and found that this day has long passed,

*for it's, in fact, this continuation I'm in today, an early version
of tomorrow.*

Let me get up, take a shower, and get some sleep.

Before I finish this day, I'll have to rest.

*I begin and end any given day tomorrow, and most of my
yesterday's only end when I fall asleep the day after or is it before
the day that follows…*

I'm quite tired."

Applause fills the room, fingers popping in rhythm, as the
lights fade to black.

I think I understand what Open Mic is saying. Cleo is
talking about a redbone with blue eyes. I'm checking her out,
too, wondering if she was born with eyes like that or if they
are contacts. I see she's walking away, and I hope Cleo said
nothing crazy. It doesn't seem like she's walking away mad.
Cleo looks at me and then follows her to the back, signaling
me to follow him. Right now, I'm thinking, *We shouldn't be
going back there. I'm almost sure it's not okay for us to be backstage.*
There are a couple of doors, and he doesn't know which one
she went through.

Cleo seems to think she went through this door over here.

"What do you want from her? She walked away."

"You got it wrong man, she was paged."

"Is that what she told you? I guess that was a polite enough goodbye, don't bother me. I see how you could have mixed up that message."

"Right, whatever, she said her name is Flo; I'm just trying to get this number before we have to make this run."

I wonder, *What run?*

Cleo checks the doorknob and finds it locked with an electric keypad. He knocks, but no one comes to the door.

I tell him, "Let's go if it's locked. You can catch her on another night."

He wants me to try, so I do. I'm pushing a few of the buttons on the keypad. In fact, I use the same numbers we have at work to get into the overnight letter drop box. I turn the knob and it opens.

Three or four people are sitting in the break room and Flo turns around without a smile.

I apologize. "This looks like a bad time."

Since I open the door and walk in first, they don't see Cleo behind me. I can sense a little tension. Before words start flying, Cleo steps from behind me. Flo sees him and smiles, to my surprise and relief. They realize we're not there to cause any trouble.

Cleo starts his apology for breaking in on them, asking if he can get a quick minute with Flo.

Flo asks if he can wait.

Cleo apologizes again. "No. I just got paged, so I need to bounce. I didn't want to leave without asking for your number. In my defense, I knocked, but no one answered, and it was open."

Flo says to him, "The door was closed and locked."

"How did we get in? We knocked." Cleo repeats the question to himself in a low voice. "How did we get in? We knocked."

Flo is talking and with a straight face says, "What? Knocked means you pick the lock and come in?"

She's looking at me. "Don't look at me."

"You opened the door."

Cleo interrupts, with a humble tone. "Look, no harm no foul right? A brother just trying to get your number. I've never seen you before and didn't want to chance not seeing you again just for not asking or being misdirected by text messages and pages out of my control. I thought we were cool out there. I'll try to catch you on a different day. At this point, I'll be hoping you don't think I'm stalking you."

Flo gets a pen and paper, writes her number, still not smiling, and hands it to Cleo. He takes it with a smile, and just as quickly, we are gone, no more words. I ask Cleo if he got paged, and he says, "No," and we laugh.

He really has to leave, and so do I. I get in my car and head home. There's no traffic. I pay the toll, drive up the mountain, and reach my front door. Everyone's asleep. I wash my face and get into bed, thanking God I've made it through another day.

The sharp, insistent blare came from the car behind me. "Okay, okay, I'm moving." He lays on the horn again. "I said, okay! Don't you see me moving?" I yell out loud, turning around to see who the impatient driver is. I blink and realize it's the alarm clock blaring at 9:11 a.m. What? The clocks aren't even set to go off, I realize as I fumble for the snooze bar. All I need is another ten minutes. My thoughts swirl, a sight and sound theater in stereo. I lay back, staring at the ceiling. I didn't even hear my wife and child leave. I must be exhausted. It's 11:30 a.m. Where did two hours go—me staring at the ceiling or dreaming of me staring at the ceiling?

"Okay, get up. Let's go," I say to myself.

Michael Jackson's "Working Day and Night" pops into my head. I take a deep breath and let it out.

I stop at Dunkin' Donuts for Turbo Ice black and two glazed donuts—actually, make that three glazed. There's nothing like cold coffee and espresso to get me going. I realize I forgot my water bottle, so I have to buy water, which I don't like doing. I have fresh well water at home. I hate being in a hurry; I always forget stuff when I rush. I punch in at work at 1:29 p.m., just a minute to spare. I could have arrived a little earlier, but it was cloudy, and I drove through some rain on the Interstate. It looks as if we might get more before the day ends. I'm not talking to anyone in particular. A few guys are standing around the punch clock, getting in the way.

A driver notices me barely making it and asks what I plan to do with all that extra time. I tell him there's no such thing as extra time—just better time management, but no actual extra time.

Another driver hopes it rains later and stops for the time being. I don't mind driving in it, working in it is a different story. Getting in and out of the van from stop to stop means briefly escaping the chill inside, only to face the rain again. With a pickup closing in two minutes, there's no time to listen to the raindrops hitting the van's metal roof, trying to gauge if the downpour will ease up. After waiting for thirty seconds, the raindrops get louder and faster. Realizing that waiting was a mistake, I jump out and dash to the front door. The rain is pouring heavily. Fortunately, the customer sees me in the van and opens the door to hand me the package. I run back to the van as the rain begins to lighten up and process the package just in time before the pickup window closes.

I still need to complete two more pickups between 4:00 and 5:00 p.m. I know I'll be five minutes late for the next one and fifteen minutes late for the other one. I'll get the pickup window changed for those two with no need to call the customers; they know I'll get their packages. I completed eight out of ten pickups. The current issue is having eight pickups scheduled for the 5:00 to 6:00 p.m. window, with the present time being 5:16 p.m. The average pickup per hour for the company is seven. The damage is done, and despite wearing a raincoat that keeps only the head and shoulders dry, the rain is now dripping all over my pants.

I tell the driver who's talking to me to be quiet. I'm trying to listen to the supervisor saying nothing.

"I'm not finished telling you how your day is going to go. Besides, he's not saying anything different from yesterday, except maybe, stay alert it's a rainy day. I've done a lot of days like this one. I'm around eighteen years in now."

"I get the picture, a messy day ahead."

The supervisor is still giving his safety briefing and most of the guys are not listening. "Blah, blah, blah paperwork, and blah, blah it looks like rain."

The driver continues to talk, almost as if to himself at this point. I've tuned him out. He goes on, "You try to stop the dripping by taking the coat off, but now it's out of the pan and into the fire. You fall back on the seat, and now a once-dry shirt is wet from the raincoat you were wearing."

"Don't wish what you see as a bad day on me."

As we walk to the first task of the day, he seems like he didn't hear a word I just said.

The driver is still talking, maybe he missed his medication. "Now the inside of the van has moisture from your wet shirt and raincoat, which then fogs up the windows. You turn on the heat because the defogger doesn't work unless there's an air-conditioner hooked to the vent system. Wait, it goes downhill from here. It takes a lot of heat to remove fog, so now it's too hot and you can hardly breathe. You let down the window and rain comes in, fogging up the front glass again. You open the window and turn down the heat, but now it's not enough to keep the glass clear, resulting in you driving slower. This is going to make you late for the appointed rounds. Stay strong it's only the third driving hour of the day, and about forty or fifty stops to go. Who knows? It may stop raining, and just be hot, and muggy."

I thank him for the rosy picture he has painted for me. "You do know this is not my first rainy day on the job? And ask your doctor to adjust your medication."

"Then you know what I mean."

"Even if I didn't, I do now. I do know I'm alive with an opportunity to make a difference in my life or the life of someone else. It's going to be a good day. I'm hoping for a truck with air-conditioning, and then I can go about my day even though it may be wet. In a controlled climate I'll have clear windows that I may witness the madness this day can bring."

Now the driver can hear me talking and respond to my inner peace.

"Right, can I get some of those happy pills from you?"

I guess I'm dreaming, for in the distance I see an air-conditioned van approaching.

He asks, "How can you tell?"

"I could tell you, but then I would have to have someone kill you."

"Oh, you can't do the deed yourself, not bad enough?"

"Who am I? Extra good. I'm an owner, not a player."

"Okay, okay, I smell you."

I'm guessing he doesn't think I'm serious because I'm smiling. We go our separate ways, laughing and pointing.

He says, "You the man."

"No, I'm the man next to the Man." Meaning, I stand with God. I wonder where that saying came from?

Shaking my head, I watch him walk away. Listen, air-conditioned vans are becoming scarce. Here are a few things to look for when searching for one. Those who pay attention to details can easily spot them. It's getting harder as the shop makes all the vans look identical. In the early days of the merger, DHL vans were white with radio antennas, while ABX vans were gray without antennas because they didn't have radios. Additionally, the trim was different: DHL vans had white or silver bumpers, mirrors, and wheels, while ABX vans were trimmed in black. The company wanted a new look, so they painted all the vans yellow with red letters. They painted a few at a time and didn't paint the trim to save time. Now, even though all the vans are painted the same, the trim remains different. Black bumpers indicate ABX vans, while silver and white bumpers indicate DHL vans. The antennas were a giveaway until the company painted all the trim the same after vans were damaged in accidents. Drivers often make adjustments for their comfort, like modifying the vans.

Drivers take the antennas so the radio doesn't work or unplug the wires to the air compressor. They put their locks and chains on the steering wheel, leaving the van in the parking lot, sometimes for a week while they are on vacation. When I notice a van sitting in the same spot for a few days, I check with the mechanic to see if it's out of order. If it's not, I ask the supervisors to cut the lock. Sometimes the supervisors don't want to cut the locks, so I move on to another van that isn't locked down. However, I can't take these vans on the road because they often have defects, making them unusable until the shop fixes the problem. Now, the only available van is locked down with a private lock and key. At this point, the ball is in the supervisors' court. They can either cut the lock or make me wait another hour for a suitable van to come in with a day-shift driver getting off work.

I know it seems bad, but it stopped the practice of drivers thinking they have their own assigned equipment. I'm worthy of clean, dry, and good service equipment, too. Some of the vans even have cassette players and it is a better day when you can work in one of those. They say, "All good things come to an end." I don't accept that.

I pray my good thing never ends unless it ends for better, than best. I try to watch what I say or wish for. Life and death are decided by what comes out of your own mouth. When you say good things must end, you just spoke the end of good into your life. I ask you not to leave it like that, by speaking life to be better, and then best, nothing missing, nothing broken.

When the air-conditioning compressor breaks or the radios stop working, the company does not replace them. So be it. Then the supervisors start handing out keys, but I never take a bad van out on the road just to get out of the building. Eventually, they stopped giving me poor equipment. They realize I only use the best they have to offer because I give my best in return.

What is my best? When what I'm doing glorifies The Father in heaven. Gone are the days of being blamed for having a bad day because I drive a bad van off the yard, and being told I should have done a better vehicle check. In short, they could have maintained all the vehicles better. It is common sense versus spending money on million-dollar ads and Formula One race cars. Yes, the company sponsors a Formula One racing car.

I keep details of the elusive air-conditioned vans to myself. If others notice what I have done, don't tell me. You can't always tell the left hand what the right hand is doing. I'm not even going into detail on the broken safety door locks not working, and drivers getting locked in the back of the van, which could go bad on a hot day.

All is well today despite the rain and my falling asleep at a traffic light or two. Good thing cars have horns. It's communication that speaks as your voice. We say "Hi," "Watch out," "Move Up," "Move out the way," "Bait me," "Bye," and "I'm out of here." The car behind me blares its horn again. This is a long light. What day is it anyway? Half a tank of gas or two hundred fifty miles to empty, averaging 24.6 miles per gallon. The blares again. Okay, okay, I'm moving.

Let me call my wife to let her know I'll be a little late tonight due to overtime. I'll also have a couple of shots, not too strong—vodka should do it. It looks like some of the other guys had the same idea.

"What's up, Derrick?"

"You got it."

It's late so I'm thinking, *What are you doing here?* "Don't you have the seven a.m. shift tomorrow?"

"My brother, Scott, is new behind the bar tonight."

"That's your brother?"

"He's adopted."

Okay, I know Scott from playing basketball at the YMCA. I would have never put them two together as being family.

"You're right, he was with me that day."

"Listen, how 'bout a game of pool?"

I'm thinking, okay, so I can finish my drink slowly, and I'm gone. "One game, right?"

"That's cool, one game."

I can see the stage through the glass that separates the two sections of the club, so the sound of the pool balls won't disturb the show. It's cool because we still hear the acts on stage. Derrick interrupted my focus.

"If you miss this shot, I'll be winning this game."

"You'll win if you make your shot if I miss."

It is down to the wire, and the only good shot I have is not easy. I take my time and line up the shot as best I can. I need a precise cut on the eight ball. While the pockets on a pool table are relatively big, his last ball is blocking the same pocket. Too much to the right, I hit the bumper, and I haven't called the bank. Too much on the left, I chanced knocking his last ball in the pocket and setting him up for the winning shot.

Another way this can go is I miss altogether, and then he'll be set up nice for his last two shots. I pull back the stick slowly and forward with a little more than a light push. I don't think I put enough speed on the shot. It has a good cut, and now it rolls ever so slowly toward the pocket I called. It seems like it's going to stop, and a level playing field it would have, but as life goes on, today the table is leaning in my favor. The ball barely drops in the pocket. Game over.

"That was luck!" He says as if luck is never a part of the game we play.

"Skills."

"Play another and I'll let you buy me a beer."

"You lost and I have to buy you a beer? Sounds like you've had too many already."

I remind him, "We said one game. You know I would if I could. Besides, I've had enough of this day. You owe me one."

"Drive carefully."

I'm walking out of the club, and I really have had enough of this day, but it feels good to end it with a win.

Okay, it's cruise control in full effect. Just keep the car in between the lines. Yes, eyes open for the next forty miles. I'm paying the toll into the next state, and I'm 20 miles from home now. This song, "25 Miles" by Edwin Star, pops into my head, an oldie but goodie.

I reach the front door. Thank you, Lord. Not everyone made it home tonight, and I don't take it for granted. I've made it through another day in one piece.

CHAPTER 3

Something Different

An extra car in the driveway, a house guest, which means my honey will be up making breakfast for everyone in the morning. No problem, someone is always showing up, trying to get away from the city for a minute. I hope they're not asleep on the couch. I can watch a little TV and have a snack before going to bed. Most of the time, I get inside the house, kick off my shoes, then upstairs to check on my little girl. Then, I let the wife know I'm home.

Today is no different, but I hear noise as I walk up the stairs. My heartbeat is now in my throat, my feet feel heavy, and I walk softly, trying to be quiet. I've heard this kind of noise before. I can't say a word; I can hardly breathe. The heartbeat in my throat becomes a knot, so much so that I nearly choke. My mind races, spinning scenes of my life backward—a car in the driveway, her ex-husband, an old boyfriend, or someone new who doesn't know me.

As I imagine the worst, I wonder if she might be dreaming. The sounds coming from the room—could she be dreaming? "Oh, yes," she murmurs, then calls out a name too softly for me to hear. Who did she say? I slowly move toward the door, praying to God that she's just dreaming. I back up and decide to check the guest room first; no one is there. As I listen while walking through the house, I freeze when I hear another voice.

Mmm… I slip into my bedroom as quietly as possible. They are so caught up in each other that they don't realize I'm standing here—or they don't care. I feel like I could almost pass out. It's as if I'm witnessing a car accident involving people I know, and now the car is on fire. I can't help the people trapped inside, and it's too hot to get close enough to save them.

I spot the digital camera on the dresser. Good, it's facing the bed. I reach over slowly and press the record button, hoping there's enough space left on the chip to capture everything. I'll play it back for her in the morning while she's packing her things. I quietly slip out of the room and head outside to the front steps.

I sit with my face in my hands, numb and struggling to catch my breath. I notice lights on in the house across the street, but they have a pinkish glow like I'm looking through red-tinted sunglasses. I feel like I could take a life or do something that tells me I'm still alive. A car pulls up in front of the house. It's Cleo.

"What up man?" I greeted him.

"I was hoping I could catch you before you went to sleep. I guess you were in a dead zone; the call went to voicemail. Either way, I didn't want to call the house, waking people up. I found you on the front steps. What's up with you? Wife finally got tired of you not coming right home after work and forgot to change locks?"

I have a blank look on my face, watching him process what he just said. I wonder, *Was it so plain to see this coming?*

It's almost like he hears me, and he says, "What man? Say something. Let's go inside."

"No, let's not do that, she's busy. My guess is she doesn't

want to be disturbed."

"So, what? She's awake and you can't go in. Talk to me, man. What's going on?"

"She's inside. She's in there with another man."

Cleo's eyes widen. "Shut up!"

"You said talk to you, so I'm telling you."

Cleo gets quiet. I am wondering what he will say next. He looks at the house. There's worry written all over his face. "What did you do?"

"Nothing."

"Nothing! What? Okay right, let me see your hands." He grabs my hands examines them and smells them.

I recoil. "What are you doing, fool?"

"Well, if you are thinking straight, I'm checking for blood and or gasoline, that's what would be on my hands right about now."

"Can't say the thought didn't cross my mind, but my baby girl is asleep inside."

"So set the house on fire then shoot him, then shoot the wife by mistake because she screamed for help. You thought she was being trapped by a home intruder, but he was a fatal attraction for the wife, and he was setting the house on fire saying, 'If I can't have you, no one will.' They were handcuffed to the bed, and the flames were too high to get closer, then you save your little girl or something along those lines. Yes, that's what happened. Right, or no? Okay no. Right so, you're just going to do nothing?"

"I took pictures."

"You took pictures? What? They didn't hear or see you standing over them taking pictures?"

I was shaking my head.

"*Damn*, they were getting busy like that?"

"Yes and no. You see, we have this digital camera, but we never use it, so it sits on the dresser collecting dust. You can take single photos or hold the button down for 1.5 seconds and act like a video recorder until you press the button again or the chip fills up and then turns off automatically. It was already facing the bed, all I had to do was reach over and hold the button down a second or two and I backed out. I think I'm going to be sick."

Cleo grabs my arm and pulls me up. "Not here, stand up. Come on, man, and stand up. You're done with this piece, right?"

"You're right I'm done. I can't see myself having any peace of mind here. I figured I'd play the tape on the flat screen while she's packing her stuff."

"Good for you. Let me help you to your car."

I walk toward the car and realize I'm barefoot. "Wait… my shoes, my keys. I can't go back in there. I'll die and want to take them with me."

Cleo sits me down. "I'll get them."

"My shoes are right as you walk in, black low tops. The keys are on the stand next to the door."

"Okay, let's just get you into the car first."

I'm sitting in the driver's seat with my head down on the steering wheel, thinking, *Is this really happening?* She could have said something, or maybe she did, and I wasn't listening. I remember us saying if we started falling apart, we would talk about it. I guess actions speak louder than words. Yes, I hear you now loud and clear. Who is this guy? I suppose I'll find out soon enough.

Cleo walks out of the house and down the stairs. "Here you go—keys, shoes, water bottle."

I didn't ask for the water bottle. I needed a drink.

Cleo informs me that my fingerprints are on the bottle. It's my house, my fingerprints are everywhere. "What did you do, Cleo?"

"Nothing, I know how you drink it, and you need it, and if I was in this situation, I would be trying to cover tracks of deeds, even if I could never be held responsible. I would be out of my mind right now; the water was a reflex. We are good, right?"

"It's cool. Where are we going?"

He tells me we are going back to the club. I let him know that I'm not of mind to drive. "I can't, that's over an hour's drive."

"What? You're going to stay here? Man up, let's go."

"Okay, what have I got to lose?"

We drive back to the club. I keep my eyes on the red lights

on the back of his car, thinking that's all I need to do to stay on track. As I drive, my life plays out before me, like a movie on my windshield—the good, the bad, and thoughts of my baby girl.

We're back at the club now. I still have my work shirt on.

"Where the blood come from?"

I told him I didn't know. Further examination reveals my nose bleeding. The phrase, "Pressure buss a pipe," comes to mind. I guess a lot is on my mind right now.

"I can't go back into the club like this."

"No extra clothes in the backseat or trunk? Looks like you got everything else in there. Man, you really need to clean out your car."

"You're right, I should be doing a lot of things. Right now, a shirt is what I need."

"I got it—a long sleeve with collar, black tee, and a perfect fit."

"Prefect, put it on, and let's go into the club."

"Can we fall back on ordering me around?"

"Thought you needed some help."

"I do."

Cleo suggests, "Let's go in and have a drink, and call your wife. Tell her you are helping me with some girl problems."

"What? You've got girl problems? I have girl problems. That's why you came out of the house, to talk to me about a girl? Must be important. Let me guess, you like gray eyes, right? I thought you were helping me."

I guess as women go, I'm done for a minute.

Talking to myself out loud, I wait for the wife to pick up the phone. "What about my daughter? I guess she'll be okay. Hopefully, she won't be able to put two and two together, thinking, why is this strange man walking around the house? Hopefully, the wife will have the sense to avoid contact with her and him or does she already know him?" The answering machine picks up. It figures. "Hello, it's me, pick up. Okay, I guess you're busy or sleeping. Anyway, I'll be a lot later tonight. Cleo wants to know if I can talk to him about some girl issues since he notices the great relationship we have. I'm trying to give him some brotherly advice. I'll be home as soon as I'm done."

As you might expect—or maybe not—I'm drinking more than I usually would. I see myself as a bit above average, but here I am in a predictable situation with no guide on what to do next. A husband spends more time away from home than he should, and a vulnerable wife fills the void with someone else. When the husband finds out, he heads to the bar. Seems pretty average to me.

Now that I've had too much to drive home, why would I? There's no home there; home is gone. What's Open Mic talking about?

Man, it's hot in here.

We're going to die you and I

It's too late; no one's going to rescue you or me

Tears won't put out the fire
It only becomes fuel to the flame
So, let's make the most of this moment
Let this be the new and final thing
A slow dance in a burning house
It's hot, it's real, it's sad, it's done, and my heart is broken.
My heart
Right now, these are happy thoughts
Can't seem to put out my mind what I saw go down. It's a long, hard, sad, bad day.

Am I alive? Am I in a relationship and hope has been denied?

The two wrapped around each other, together under and over, even then over again, as the dance flickered out and I mark this day [the moment Trust died].

Finger snapping and the lights fade to black on the man, who sits behind the cloth, with a guitar he doesn't play. What do I do with myself now? My mind is in a daze, and I'm already missing that part of my life. Only a few hours have passed, and I can hardly feel my heartbeat. The reality of my home. It's funny—if I hadn't seen the deed with my own eyes, I don't think anyone could have warned me, that I was walking toward the valley of the shadow of death. We walk and talk of life and love and discuss like any other couple, and the thought of us becoming part of the fifty percent who don't make it never crossed my mind. One can roll the dice or play the cards dealt. Flipping a coin or praying are also options.

What do I have at the end of each day? I want to fall on

the positive side of the numbers. "We will stay together, our love will never die, and I love you 'til the end of time." Sure, I've said these words to someone else before, but I married her. I belong to her, and she to me, and now to another. I think of it all, and it puts me in a special place of so much pain in my brain, and my heart beats slowly. Oh my God, they keep me from dying. It seems natural to just let go—do I let go? What about the rest of my life? Will it be less now? Will we fall short of the mark? Forever ever, forever ever, I'm screaming my head off and the room shakes all inside me, and I'm beside myself. Everything is shifting, and it's raining, and my daughter. Is she mine? How can I know for sure without a blood test? It's the birth of mistrust, and how long is the lie? What should I tell my daughter about a blood test? Do I use hair? The truth will come soon enough as the dark gives way to the light. Nothing matters; my soul cries out. What kind of wrong is this? People shouldn't have to go through this kind of deception, ever. I feel as if I could roll up into a ball here on the floor and pass away.

A song on the radio by Robin Thicke adds the soundtrack to the hurt, and as soundtracks go, I live a little piece of it each time I hear some song.

Cleo suggests I crash at his place tonight. "Or do you want me to take you to a hotel? Leave your car here at the club." He thinks it will be okay.

We get to Cleo's place, and I flop down on the couch.

Coach leather, nice. I've had enough to drink, I'm thinking. Cleo has a nice place.

"Thanks." I guess I said that out loud.

"Yes, you did."

"I suppose I'm talking out loud instead of thinking to myself."

"Yes, you are."

I let him know I see the company has been good to him.

Cleo, with no emotion, questions me. "So, let me get this straight. You can have a three-thousand-square-foot house, with wall-to-wall carpet, a three-car garage, and twelve-foot windows. Good luck cleaning those, by the way. All brick, with a view of Friday night fireworks from the amusement park, and I just spend all my money on wine, women, song, guns, cars, and gambling?"

"Yes."

"You're half right, but I like it like that. I've tried it the way you just tried it and pretty much came up with the same way you're headed. How do you know I don't have what you have somewhere?"

"I don't know and I'm not judging you. I'm just saying, it's nice what you've done with what the company pays you."

"Why are you trippin'? Do you have a house somewhere?"

Cleo calms down. "You're right. I'm trippin'

"I guess you forgot that DHL isn't the only thing we do for money."

"I know you cut hair on the side."

Cleo's comment raises my eyebrow. "Those bumps on the head really have you turned around at times. Hope you snap out of it soon."

That statement about the extra money I make woke me up a little, for I had no idea what he was talking about.

"What about the oil paintings, and statues, and the grandfather clock? Nice, but a little strange—the clock is counting backwards."

"Yes, I picked it up at a specialty shop."

"The clock is counting down to what? Now who's trippin'?"

"Think you're up to a little extra money tonight, which brings me back to the other reason I came by your house tonight. I got a call from the man."

"What bump on the head?"

Cleo hears me talking to myself again and answers, "One was a letter container that hit you hard enough to knock you out about a month ago."

"Can't say I remember the details of that situation right now."

"You told me the doctor told you that you may have some memory loss at times and, for the most part, you're as okay as you're going to be. So, you think it's okay to make this money or not?"

"Sure, what do you need me to do?"

"I got security, you got the locks, as always."

I'm thinking, *Like always? How many times have we done this? Do we get paid? And if so, where am I hiding my cut?*

So, we pull up to the riverfront, where rows and rows of freight train box cars stacked two cars high on top of each other, blocking the view of the city lights across the river. Cleo gets out of the car and looks around; one hand inside the pocket of a long trench coat. He looks back and gives me the all-clear sign, then moves forward and gives me the number of the container we're looking for. I begin by looking at the barcodes that identify the cargo of the box cars. I go through about eleven or twelve cars before realizing the sequence in which two cars are stored on the dock.

Cleo is never more than twenty or thirty feet away. I'm finally at a matching barcode to the one I hold in my hand. I could see from the car even before I got out, the large locks that secured the doors of the box cars. I reach into the bag of tools Cleo gave me. I left mine in my car parked at the club. He also lets me in on an observation of his, that I never use anything in my bag of tricks, so his bag is as good as any. I ask, "How do you think I get the lock open?"

"I never need to know the magic behind the trick. All I know is the job gets done. We get paid. That's all I have to say about the horse that bears gifts."

"What are you talking about? I need to talk to you about the get-paid part you mentioned. I'm curious to know what you have to say about that."

"A conversation for later, after we finish this job," he says.

I take a quick inventory of the items inside the bag Cleo has given me: bolt cutters, lock pick kit, acid, plastic explosives, and gloves. I put on the gloves after putting the bag on the ground. I grab the lock to brace myself as I kneel, and the lock opens. I don't know why, I haven't touched it with a tool. I take the lock off and put it in the bag and we walk back to the car.

"Why did you take the lock?"

"I want to see if it is broken. All I did was use it to balance myself, and as I went to one knee, it opened."

Cleo tells me, "You always say that or some other excuse like that. You didn't want anyone to examine the lock to see what method you used to open it, or maybe the dock worker forgot to lock it, or some version of all that. Whatever man, you don't want me in your bag of tricks, and that's cool. I suppose if I knew what you know, I wouldn't need you now, would I? On the other side of the same coin, I can't see you doing what I do either, or would you bother? Let's go."

I'm perplexed. "That's it? What about the cargo inside the box?"

"Not our problem, we're done. We are not getting paid to see or carry whatever is inside that box."

"Don't you want to know? Let's go see."

Cleo tells me in a way that makes me think I should know why we are not looking inside that box. "It's not that kind of party. It's like this, greed kills, and a lot of times sadness comes with knowledge. The powers that be know we don't need to know any more than what they tell us, it protects all of us, and if for some reason you find out, don't tell me. We're on a need-to-know basis. Like, the people who are assigned to pick up the cargo. They don't know who opened it. Then consider our cut for the part we have in this little play. Is it more than enough? They know we know our limit; we need to let them continue to think that."

"Don't you want to know if it's worth your time, your freedom, your life?"

Cleo's looking at me as if I have two heads. "You really trippin', but okay, I'll play. What if we look and it's empty because someone is going to put something inside, and since we are being watched most of the time, if not all the time, just for looking in the box, we forfeit our pay? That would be a $200,000-dollar test we failed. At a fifty-fifty split, do you really need to know what could be or not be?"

"We're going to make $100K each?"

"Is that all you heard?"

"No, I heard you, but it became hard to process after all the numbers."

Departmentalization would be the operative word of the day. It's what the American government did with one hundred thousand Americans while building the most powerful weapon known at that time until they dropped it on the Japanese. In short, no one knew what they were working on. The powers that be pulled all the pieces together from all over the United States.

Cleo tells me to talk to him after work tomorrow. "We're just robbing in the hood, like in the bigger picture we are the poor. I have to keep reminding myself that you told me the doctor said you may be a little fuzzy on details at times."

We go back to Cleo's place. On the way off the dock, we pass five black midsize vehicles with tinted windows, chrome wheels, lights on high beams, all different makes and models. I'm just looking and so is Cleo. He keeps driving.

Now it's early morning when we get back to his place. He makes a beeline to his room, and I head to the couch. I guess I've been up for nineteen or twenty hours, so some sleep is in order. As I begin to pass out, my eyes pan the room and fix on the clock on the wall that counts backward. I think more than hours have passed—more like days. I drift off on this last thought.

The phone rings twice then stops. Cleo steps out of his room. "DHL is on the line. I'm next on the call list after they called you and got your answering machine. I told them you were here. They said we both can go in early if you want."

We both go in, and I don't know how much sleep I get—I lost track some time ago. Try to keep up. We pull into work around 9:30 a.m. I'm about to get the items I need for my route when the thought crosses my mind to speak with my daughter before I get started since I won't see her until tomorrow morning. I put all her mother's stuff by the front door. As I finish my thoughts and walk to the phone in the break room, I'm paged to the office. An agent hands me a phone. "It's your daughter."

"Good morning, River."

"Good morning, Daddy."

"Hey, baby, how are you doing today? I was just thinking of you and was on my way to the phone to call. Is everything okay?"

"Well, the phone woke me up, and I heard the answering machine pickup and I heard someone say 'I'm calling from DHL to see if you wanted to start work early today.' I didn't see your car and Mommy won't answer me or unlock the bedroom door to let me in your room."

I don't know what to think. "Right, okay, well sweetie, just turn on the TV and watch your shows. Daddy is on his way home now."

"I'm hungry."

"Get some milk and cereal. I'm on my way."

"Okay."

She doesn't sound panicked, I'm thinking. I'll tell my supervisor what's going on with this call and let him know I have an emergency at home, and I have to leave.

I need a car. Cleo. I'll ask dispatch if he has left the building, and they say he's already gone. I call him on my cell to ask to use his car. No answer, straight to voicemail, so I leave a message. I go to his car, open the door, and sit down. It's a push-button start. I press the button and it starts, and I'm off. I try to call again—a strong signal. It's ringing loud and clear, too loud, like it's in the seat next to me. I leave another message to let him know I have his car, so he shouldn't worry about his car being stolen. I then call dispatch to ask Derrick to send him a message with the details.

CHAPTER 4

One hour later, I'm home. River is sitting in front of the TV and there is an empty bowl and spoon next to her, plus cookies.

"Hi, Daddy."

I get a big hug and kiss from her.

"Hey, Miss River, my sugar. You okay?"

"Yes."

"I see you ate a little. Did you get enough?"

"Yes."

"What did you have to eat?"

"See look, I had milk and cereal."

"And?"

"And cookies."

I wonder if she remembers how many cookies she had.

So, I ask.

"Three or four or five. Can I have one more?"

"I think you've had enough for today."

"Okay, I want to see Mommy."

"Okay, me first. Go watch your shows, and I'll go wake up Mommy for you."

My mind is racing, and my heart is beating up in my throat. *Be cool, man, be cool. The strange car is still in the driveway.* River sits and I start up the stairs. I'm feeling the madness now, the disrespect, the nerve to have someone still here in the morning, just in case I missed the show last night. Maybe they saw me come in and decided to face the music. They must be crazy or stupid to want to be here when I arrive. As if I would not react. Maybe she feels I wouldn't care at all, or they must be on drugs to develop a larger set of balls. In this state, I could kill him for trespassing, say he broke in. They just don't care. I open the door and there are pools of blood everywhere and on just about everything it seems. I'm guessing they're dead. I look at the camera, bloody, but not over the lens. I leave it, hoping it can show I didn't do this, but who did, and are they still here? I call out to River. I can hardly move without tracking in blood. I can go no further.

I hear my daughter walking up the stairs. I turn around, walk out of the room, and close the door behind me.

She cries out, "Mommy, Mommy!" I jump back into my skin and pick her up, hoping she doesn't see much.

"Is Mommy going to be okay?"

"I hope so. Let's go get you ready for school and I'll come back to check on Mommy. She's cool, okay?"

I am getting River ready for school and grabbing extra clothes for her. She won't be back in this house for some time.

As we are walking out the door, River turns around and yells up the stairs. "See you later, Mommy. The Lord watches between me and thee while we are absent, one from another. Amen."

We start down the steps to Cleo's car, and she notices the stains on the glass, a strange car in the driveway, and quizzes me on both. I give her short answers.

"I don't know, and I guess Mommy needed to borrow a car to get home like I did. See Mr. Cleo's car there?" I'm glad she doesn't ask me what's going on with my car. I put on some jazz music and take her to school. She falls asleep like she does on a normal day, but this day is far from normal.

My head is spinning. I'm guessing the intruder tracked blood out of the house on his or her shoes as they were leaving. Now I've tracked blood into Cleo's car, taking River to school.

I drop her off and call the police, explaining briefly what has happened. I am told a patrol unit will wait at my home until I get there.

The police and I go into the house. I point them up the stairs towards the room. They tell me to stay by the door, so I sit in a folding chair we keep by the door for guests to take off their shoes before walking around the house. They see the bloody stairs, and as I sit looking up the stairs, I notice no dry blood from last night, just the tracks I made this morning.

Could I have stepped in the same spots left behind from last night? Or will they think I made the spots because I did it and made tracks when I picked River up and left the house? This doesn't look good for me because they will notice sooner or later the tracks to River's room, where I gathered extra clothes for her to wear later. They've already noted the stains in the grass and sidewalk. Why didn't River mention blood on the steps and carpet she walked by? She's pretty sharp when it comes to things out of place. As I think back, I didn't notice blood as I walked into the house—not until I opened the bedroom door. *Okay, get your truth and stick to it.*

It's like I black out; I have to remind myself to inhale and exhale. Once they're at the room door, it's locked, and I tell them the key is over the door. They take a step in and stop. One officer pivots, weapon drawn, and ready to shoot. Some position I'm in. The other is now stepping backward, weapon drawn. One officer is pointing his weapon at me now, and the other officer is back and forth with his, then back to the bedroom. I know what they see, but I did not expect them to react that way. I brought them here. They act like I'm the intruder. One officer yells, "Don't move, sir!" I'm hoping I don't get shot at this point. They walked backward down the stairs toward me, looking in all directions.

Other police are coming in from outside, all looking at me as if I am crazy enough to run. One officer on the steps is shaking, and I can feel what's going to happen next—the perfect storm. All that has to happen now is someone loses their footing, and then the two of them tumble down the stairs with their fingers on the triggers of the guns. I get grazed in the neck. I turn and slam my face and head into the wall, and I'm out for the count.

I wake up in the back of a squad car, one arm cuffed to the door. I watch as more police cars pull up—some marked some unmarked—ambulance, coroner van, and I fade to black again.

"I'm exhausted."

I wake up to a soft-spoken voice. "Wake up. Daddy, everything's going to be okay."

A car door closes as an officer returns to his seat inside the patrol car. I open my eyes slowly and just a crack so they won't know I'm awake. The cop in the driver's seat looks directly at me but can't tell I'm conscious. My eyes stay fixed, my pupils focused with no motion, as if I staring right through him. I can't see the second officer because of the angle of my head against the window and my lifeless trance. I hear them. I can see the side of one's face and hear the voice of the other. Fear has a scary grip on them both. The driver is sweating and commenting on how he can't believe what he saw.

"All the blood."

The other driver agrees. "I hear you. I had to get out of there."

They go on talking. "The writing on the wall, 'An angel of God.' What is that all about?"

"That's just what we need, another fan of Jesus, talking about he's doing the work of God."

"Or a she."

"Do you think a woman could have decapitated a body without a weapon?"

"No weapon found?"

"Not yet."

"Do you think a man could have pulled the head off a body with nothing to cut with?"

"No, I don't."

"Vengeance is mine, saith the Lord."

"More writing on the wall?"

"Yep."

I'm thinking, I know what I saw last night, and today I find an angel of the Lord has answered quickly with judgment, without grace, or mercy, and out of patience. Thank you, God, Who can forgive us of our trespasses, as we forgive those who trespass against us. It seems like I looked over the fact that a head is missing from the body, and I'm glad I didn't see that. It explains all the blood. I don't know if I should be happy or sad.

Father God, in heaven, I come to You with a broken heart. I need You now more than ever, to keep me in Your perfect peace. I've been handed this bitter cup. Why? My soul cries, "Why?"

The Word of the Lord spoke to me. "Your spirit knows that I am a very present help in times of trouble, and My grace is sufficient. I will have mercy on whom I will have mercy and compassion on whom I will have compassion." He cast upon them the fierceness of His anger, wrath, indignation, and trouble by sending evil angels among them. He made a path to His anger; He spared not their souls from death but gave their lives over to the pestilence. They profess they know God, but in their works, they deny Him, being abominable and disobedient, and unto every good work reprobate. And even as they did not like to retain God in their knowledge, God gave them over to a reprobate mind to do those things which are not convenient. Children of wrath, this is the calamity you see today.

After that crazy scene at my house, this is no longer a home. The police took me to the station for questioning. I tell my story just as I want them to hear it or as I saw it happening. For instance, not me coming home and seeing them in bed and yet staying cool enough to turn on the camera, but me calling from the club a second time to say, "I've had too much to drink and I'm going to sleep it off at a friend's house near the club. It's Cleo; you have his number if you need me." Then I get called into work from there and later receive a call from my daughter, asking me to come home, where I find the scene and call the police. The truth gives me motive and opportunity, and I'm unsure if I can convince a jury that I'm incapable of beheading a body. Who knows what anyone is capable of after alcohol and discovering infidelity?

That Cleo came by the house isn't good, which implicates him. What could two people accomplish in that situation? What a mess? I hope my little timeline works out. It will be harder to convince a jury of my innocence if someone finds the holes. I just have to stick to my story forever. The truth will surely land me in jail, trying to find answers from behind bars. I'm innocent even if I have to tell a lie to prove it. Yes, the truth will make me free. Instead of being in jail in bondage to the lie, I'd rather freely walk the streets.

After my first message saying I'll be going to the club and coming home after some drinks, I twist it into having too many drinks to drive and leaving my car at the club to sleep it off at Cleo's place, which is nearby. The second message establishes this. While I write this tale in my statement to the police, I'm thinking I sure hope to see Cleo before the police do. He told me to make the second message, so I'm thinking he already knows how this should play out from the start. I'm hoping I can reenact the facts of the event as he may see it, so it would be good to know we'll be on the same page.

The detectives take me to where I say I left my car. I'm trippin', hoping no one decided to steal my car last night. It's a relief to see it's where I said I parked it. The truth is, I did have a few too many drinks, and I could have totally misplaced a car. The story is checking out so far, and they release me with the "Don't leave town anytime soon" line and say they'll be in touch.

Before they drive away, I flag them down and ask them to take me back to my house to pick up Cleo's car. This would give me time to settle down. I don't feel I can drive; I am still a little shaken up by recent events. I tell them I can catch a ride with Cleo. They give one another a look and agree. While riding with the detectives, I give Cleo a call, saying I'll be waiting in his car until he is off work. This puts me and my shoes and the blood that would have been on my shoes last night in his car right now—if I did it, I don't know.

After waiting for several minutes, I ask the detectives, who are now waiting with me in their car within sight, to take me to Cleo's apartment so I can lie down. Besides, I can't go back to my house. They agree, exchanging that same look as before. Now, traces of blood are in his apartment, too, as I just tracked it there.

I take a second to close my eyes, and my thoughts go straight to my River. What to do with her? What do I tell her about her mommy? I know some version of the truth will be known one day; hopefully, she'll be old enough to understand the details.

I'm not used to living alone and taking care of a child. I already know I'm going to need help with River, but who? I know who I can call, but it's only been a few days, and knowing some of what she's going through makes me feel weird.

Joy called my mother to update her on her husband, who was very sick and has now passed away. My mother and Joy agreed that it wasn't a surprise; when his sickness took a turn for the worse, there were no good days after that. Since my mother and I talk regularly, I knew I should have called Joy to express my condolences. The fact is, I know about the burden she no longer has to bear. The word on the street is her husband died from lung complications. I know different. In light of that whole truth, it was good news in some respects, but that is another story.

Later in the same week, my wife and her adulterer have been found murdered in my house. I still have to ask. I have no other place to go, so I ask Joy if she can keep River. After going over the details with Joy, we say, "Sorry," to each other, and she agrees, saying it will be a refreshing change. She adds that taking care of River will help her process her situation. This is a chance to care for the living instead of the dying.

Joy is someone I've known since I was thirteen years old, my first girlfriend. We met while I was working on my paper route. My best man takes credit for that moment because it was his paper route that had grown too big for him to cover. We were kids and thought, like most first loves, we would be married and stay together forever and a day. I remember the first time our lips touched; it was soft like a stick of butter in a warm room. That was the high school kiss. The fourteen-year-old smack on the lips was like having a walking, talking, glazed donut, my favorite treat. We discovered that life doesn't march up through time as smoothly as we imagined, and neither does happiness ever after, or does it?

After her, we can only answer that question for ourselves with the question of how we view abundance: half full or running over. I must say, I've known a few young ladies and some well enough to say I've been in love more than I care to mention. The flames will remain nameless to protect me. I sometimes stare into the fireplace, separated from being consumed by the heavy glass door. I remember my emotional pain and sometimes physical encounters with a broken heart. I consider the damage I may have caused. I tread lightly, thinking my decisions had no consequences. I look in the mirror and see a person I had not known I had become. In light of that, I offer my sincere apology for my behavior. I was a boy doing grown-man things, not fully understanding the actions that would reverberate forever.

Having children out of wedlock is not very responsible, and the decision to abort was selfish. Yes, I'm forgiven by the Blood of Jesus. I cannot forget, and I live with that. I remember and wonder what those babies could have become. I thank God for those who made it through the killing fields. In my mind, I've paid that debt with a pound of my own flesh. I thought God had blessed me with a child; my wife and I had a hard time conceiving. This child died in the womb. Okay, enough of that, back to Joy.

As life would have it, we married, but not to each other. I let go, then she let go of that part of our childhood dream. Over the years, we stayed in touch, so the girlfriend became the little sister I never had. The relationship was complete with visits to the parents when one of us was in town. We were just around the corner from each other. Now, after all this time, we still have each other to help with messy situations. She sent me the Whitney Houston and CeCe Winans duet, "Count on Me." I asked, and she said, "Not to worry." She would even pick River up from school to stay with her. I thank God for her being a blessing to me.

Now that I have another base covered, my mind goes to that run with Cleo later that night. I'm thinking if we're getting paid, then where is my cut? Where is my plush apartment, or am I living above my legal means in the three thousand square feet house? Things that make you go, *hmmm*.

It's early, but the club is open. I sat down, and in came Cleo. He says he left work early after working a straight eight, something union workers are not supposed to do. He manages a ride to the club and remembers I have his car. He's surprised but not really, wondering why I didn't ask. I told him I tried, but the phone rang in his car. I left a message anyway on his phone.

"I asked the dispatch to tell you to call your phone for the message. I guess Derrick dropped the ball on that one."

I ask him to check his phone. He wasn't trippin' on that, but he does need to call the police to let them know he found his car since he reported it stolen. I give him the details of why I took his car in such a hurry, which raises an eyebrow. He says the police haven't spoken to him yet. We have a few drinks while I tell him everything I said and did with the police. After we get those facts straight, he starts talking to me about the next big job. We will learn more later tonight.

"I guess I'm hanging out with you. My place is still a crime scene."

"Cool."

Now it's back to his place for some much-needed sleep. We have a long night ahead. I jump in my car and follow with a lot on my mind.

I shower, shave, and change clothes I just happen to have in the trunk of my car: black jeans, a black sleeveless t-shirt, and black long sleeves with the word "Gorillas" stitched vertically onto one pant leg. The same words appear on the collar of the long black sleeve, black tread on both. I wear Gorilla wear—my first commercial.

We drive thirty-two miles, and we're there. I haven't been to this part of town before. I'm trying to keep up with Cleo, who drives too fast for me to see all the street signs. The building faces a major expressway, with three lanes in both directions. Okay, I see the numbers, four, five, four. That's easy to remember because the 76ers took the Basketball World Championship with Dr. J and company: first round in four games, second round in five games, third round in four games. I played those numbers, straight and box, in the Illinois lottery and won four hundred fifty-four dollars. That's when the show began, not in LA.

It's a very wide building, not too tall—five stories high and about two or three times as wide. Imagine that. The front of the building is all glass with a gold tint. I can see the lights from the expressway reflected on the glass. Inside is dark, as expected after hours. We park and walk to the glass doors. I grab the handle; it's open. I let Cleo go in first. The lighting on the floor is like something you'd see in a movie theater, creating a similar effect. I can see where I'm going but not much else. There are shadows and profiles, like having a flashlight shining under your chin.

Cleo and I are not the only crew here. We are all around a jogging track with glass walls, looking down onto a basketball court. There's a long table set up in the middle of the floor, with seats for thirty people. I think this setup is designed so that the powers that be can recognize some of the players but not all. They can only see the person next to them and, as far as their eyes can focus, across the room or table in the dark space, with lighting only on the floor.

The table below has men in dark suits sitting and more men with darker suits standing behind them. Only the people in your sight know you have a part, no one knows all the parts. We are a piece of the puzzle, pawns trying to become queens and kings. My guess on some of the profiles I see at the table is from what I see on the news. I don't keep up with world events as I should, but after tonight, I'll be paying more attention.

A car pulls up outside. The glass that faces the expressway is behind us. It's a 1930 Model J American-built Duesenberg, estimated to be worth around $1.5 million at auction. A man wearing a military uniform, not American, gets out of the car. Dark-suited men with turbans for headdresses accompany him. My first thought is Saddam Hussein, but only God really knows. Whoever it is has arrived after everyone else and is leaving before us all, after fifteen minutes of talking. The body language makes me believe this person is upset with the current arrangement. The man with him also leaves, walking backward. Others in the room include heads of state, both present and past, and people in high places, as they say. They are the ones who have exalted themselves and are thus named "the powers that be," along with the people who control them.

The meeting carries on for another forty-five minutes. "We will be in contact concerning your involvement," the man announces. We leave through a separate door from the others at the table. When we get outside, limousines are parked fifty yards away.

I have questions for Cleo. "What's up, man? What are we into?"

"If you don't remember, you don't want to know. Let me say that our game just went to the next level. We've been invited to a big game, confirmed by us living through the night. It's the kind of thing that will allow us to make this our last job, one way or another."

"As if we could just walk away from the game."

Now that we know another game is being played, one that isn't played by the average person, they know we know.

I'm thinking to myself, *All I've seen on TV about organized crime and gangsters, I have come to the conclusion that the average person doesn't have a clue.* This is gangster tenfold, which is very different from gangster times ten.

What's the difference? Two times ten is twenty, and two tenfold is two thousand forty-eight. Two becomes four, four becomes eight, eight becomes sixteen, and so on. We can even look at something as simple as folded paper. The paper becomes harder to cut or tear apart. What of the things of God? One puts a thousand to flight, and two puts ten thousand to flight. We see these phrases in the Bible, some thirty, some sixty, some one-hundred-fold. I'm saying this is how God says He will compensate us for our obedience to Him.

Am I a chess piece being moved by the hand of man? Who is the man that moves the pieces? Am I winning? And if so, where's my cut?

We leave the meeting without much being said between us. We see the other players in the game, and I'm thinking, *What piece of the puzzle am I?* As we walk to our cars, only face recognition, no names; I know no one else's name. I know of Cleo, for the Word says, "*The heart is desperately wicked, who can know it.*" Like my nephew says, "I know you, but I don't know you."

"See you back at the club?"

"Why not? Where else am I going? Just got paid, it's Friday!" I encourage myself.

I follow him back to the club and go left in my own mind. My car just floats along on the CD mix: David Benoit's "Floating," Grover Washington, Jr.'s "Knucklehead," and George Howard's "When Summer Comes." I could be moving sideways for all I know. I can't feel the road under my wheels.

My wife is dead, along with her adulterer, who is missing his head in dismemberment. My house is a crime scene. How long has it been this way? When did she stray, or was that the first time? Am I always out late, and in doing so brought this on myself? Is this the damage left behind from my movement through this underground? Selective memory edits bring about blank spaces, and then there's River and now Joy. I'm having everything to think about.

The authorities think I did it. Tim Bowman's "Sweet Sunday" and Walter Beasley's "Good Morning" play in the mix. The car door closes with a good thump. My eyes move across the parking lot and now back again at the club—looks like the regular crowd. I pay a small fee to enter and make my way directly to the bar. The atmosphere is lively, with a cheerful crowd, the clinking of glasses, and the pleasant sound of ice cubes. In this moment, I can almost momentarily forget that my life has undergone a significant change.

A part of it is done and gone forever. I will sit by and watch River grow, hoping she will have a chance to start anew. She will encounter fast turns, some expected and others unexpected. I pray that God will guide her and help her overcome any rough patches she may encounter. I hope she stays true to her teachings and avoids anything that goes against her beliefs. If she must make choices, I hope she proceeds with caution, fully aware of the consequences that may follow. It's important to live a planned and accurate life, and when faced with difficult decisions, choose the option that leads to a better outcome. Sometimes, a second chance isn't an option, and sometimes, even one chance is too many.

Unfortunately, I do not have enough time at this place to be on a first-name basis with the owner. Tonight, she's behind the bar. I guess someone called in sick.

"Ms. Bartender! I'll have a Mountaineer."

"Is that a shot of Wild Turkey and Kahlua with cream or milk, right? We have milk."

"Milk is good."

"Coming right up."

The announcer says good evening to everyone. "At this time, I bring to the stage, Flooooo!"

Everyone's fingers are snapping as she begins to sing her face off! And yes, she's the definition of a triple threat— she can sing, she's beautiful, and she's a poet. The crowd is captivated, falling into a trance at the sound of her voice. Then, all too soon, her performance comes to an end. The curtain lowers and the lights dim, as if creating a moment of silence to reflect on what was just shared. Gradually, the club lights start to glow again, casting a soft ambiance on the scene. The energy of the place resumes as waiters serve their customers once more.

Where have I been? What has brought me here, and where will I find what I lack? Do I want back what was taken, or did I lose it due to my own negligence? If the latter, from whom shall I seek compensation? God has the answers. As profound as the paper is fragile, I remain still, like ink on the aforementioned paper. I shake it off, enjoy a drink, and divert my thoughts elsewhere. Miles Davis, the legendary King of the Blues, fills the background with his iconic track, "So What," which happens to be the first on the CD.

The glasses clink with the sound of ice, while conversations, either trivial or profound, fill the air with an incomprehensible murmur. The crack of pool balls echoes from a nearby pool table, and a couple engage in a game of chess in a booth. Meanwhile, someone else rolls the dice, engrossed in a backgammon match.

The bartender asks, "What are you having?"

"I'm having a Mountaineer."

"What's that again?"

Because a different person is behind the bar, I explain Wild Turkey 101 proof, one shot of Kahlua or milk or cream, one shot, on the rocks.

"I've never made a drink like that," she says, "I've got it now. I'll even put it on the new mix board. Let's see who else walks in those shoes. Sorry, out of Wild Turkey."

"Okay, make that mix with any brown juice."

"Is Johnny Walker Black Label okay?"

"That's what I call an Old Mountaineer."

I scan the club, and see Cleo, signaling for me to come backstage.

"What's up?"

"I need to talk to Flo. I need you to get my back if she's not alone."

"I thought the girl's name was Denilla."

"Her stage name is Flo because of her delivery."

"Okay, it sounds like you two are serious."

"I think I'm good with her."

"I think you are moving kind of fast."

Cleo pulls at the knob. "The door is locked."

"Let me try." I jiggle the knob. "No, it's not."

"Whatever."

Cleo is through the door first this time. "What up, everybody?"

Everyone looks up with nods and figures of speech. It occurred to me that it wasn't his first time backstage, or have I lost a block of memory? He wanted to introduce me to Open Mic, but he had to make a run. Comments had been made that we look alike, Open Mic and I, the people in the room agreed. They say we all have a twin somewhere.

The people that know Open Mic best call him O.M. Our forefathers are maybe from the same tribe back in Mother Africa.

It is at that moment the room door blows open with a force that knocks people off their feet and over tables and chairs. When the smoke clears, five men in long dark green coats stand among us. I'm checking the weapons.

One of the men barks, "Empty your pockets!"

I'm like, "What? Is this a stickup?"

Green coats, more than a few. "I said empty your pockets, now!"

Before I can blink an eye, Cleo fades to black, pulls out a pair of Desert Eagles, and with these nickel-plated .9-millimeter weapons, he pops one of the green coats in the neck. Two green coats snatch up their fallen and move back out the door. At the same time, the two that remain begin spraying the room with bullets, like a scene out of *The Matrix*; all kinds of weapons are firing in different directions. It happens so fast, yet my eyes follow the path of each bullet that comes closest to me. One passes my face, then behind, as the bullet trail leads out into a life-size poster of Open Mic, right in the chest.

Two more head my way, and my mind shouts, Run, fool! The fire exit is in sight, but can I reach it? I sprint for it, jumping over two bodies. As I grab the door handle, the alarm sounds loudly, and then the gunfire stops.

I can hear the Peter Gabriel CD, *The Passion*, track nine: "Trouble."

I'm outside. *Where is my car?* There it is. I'm in, and I'm out of there. People are running here and there, and I see no signs of the men in long green coats or any typical vehicles they may have rolled up in around the parking lot. Who can see people who are not trying to be seen? It could be a car as unassuming as a brown Volkswagen Beetle. There is nothing wrong with brown. It's an ongoing rhetoric each year in honor of Black History Month in February. On the surface, it seems we're doing better. The fact is, the Bush economy has all Americans the same shade of poor or green, the new brown.

My mind is racing and tripping over itself. It's not stopping and starting the way it should, not processing information or forming a course of action. I've lost track of my friends. I hope they're okay. I'll find out soon enough. *Where am I going? Where am I going?* Before I realize it, my flight is put on auto drive, and now I'm sitting in front of my house. I see police tape across the door and the entry to the backyard. *Where is that brother's head?* I get the feeling I'll never live there again.

I walk under the tape to pick up my suits and piece of art River made, get my alarm clock, stereo, military-issued backpack, and basketball, and that's all I need. My mind floats to River. I know she's okay, and that's all I'm sure of right now. Thank God for that.

Okay now where am I really going? I don't need to burden Joy with the latest events, so it's to Cleo's place. I call first. No answer. I'm going anyway. I knock. No answer. A twist on the knob, and the door is open. Good. Also good is he's not dead on the floor from gunshot wounds. I'll sit here by the door in this leather chair. I can see most of the living space from this spot.

The clock is counting backward, with much less time remaining, it seems, from when I last saw it. Looks like a few days have passed. I don't remember seeing the chessboard the last time I was here. I look over to the game, and the setup looks like it has some extra space to play on, and a game is in progress. Interestingly, I see no extra pieces for the extra squares. Next to the game is a large remote. TV, VCR, CD, DVD, and bed up and down, *Oh, it's like that.*

I push the button down, and out of the wall, the bookcase unfolds onto the floor. It's cool. His place seemed it would have at least one bedroom, or maybe I'm in the bedroom now. I open a few doors. The first is a closet, the laundry room, and now the bedroom. Nice. So, this fold-out is for guests; I'm a guest. Cleo has pretty good taste, leather and wood on a DHL pay, and cutting hair on the side, right? *Where is my cut? Where is that guy's head?*

That's enough snooping for now. Back out to the TV and the 007 bookcase bed. I'm exhausted. What's on TV? Does it have a jazz music channel? Yes, now playing, *"I'm Covered with the Red now Fade to Black* CD by Monarch N Me, I'm The King's Kid.

CHAPTER 5

The alarm clock sounds. "Okay, okay, I'm up."

"Good morning, sweetie," my wife says. "A kiss on the forehead for you until you brush your teeth."

My precious child is not to be left out and says, "A kiss for me, too, Daddy."

"Yes, my little one, a kiss for you, too." Then I ask, "Turn off the light?"

My wife, Grace, wants to know if I'm going to be ready when she gets back.

"Ready for what?"

She yells as she has one foot out the door already. "Did you forget we have to go see the lawyer today to finalize our wills? Have you decided how long you would like to stay on life support systems?"

The door closes. It's a coin toss for me right now. I think maybe thirty days if I'm in a coma and have no quality of life when I wake up. Ninety days if I can wake up with nothing missing and nothing broken. Who's to say? Only God can say what it is to be. That's what our faith is all about. Knowing what you have before you have it. The word of God says, *"Speak life."*

Grace returns, so I ask her, "What do you think about the time you have decided on?"

"Seven days for me. I've seen enough of a bad life, and I've had my fair share of the good life. You and the baby have made my life very full. Don't want to spend much time thinking about tomorrow; it will take care of itself."

"No one does. Who knows the unknown?"

"Don't know of the unknown."

"I know."

"The ones that don't know…" she prompts me.

"No, not that they are unknown…"

"And the ones that say they know…"

"May find that the One that knows all doesn't know them."

"Stop with the double talk, back and forth," Grace tells me.

"When you let me go, we both know, without a doubt, where we will go."

"You're right, hoping what you know is true for you."

The door closes. I'm looking at the ceiling as the baby turns off the light.

Cleo steps into the apartment. I'm thinking to myself, *It seemed so real. I was talking to a lady named Grace about being on life support.*

"Cleo, good to see you're okay. What's up, man? What do you think happened at the club?"

"I think I know," Cleo says, "and I'll know more after the daily news. The news networks should have a report of what happened. If not, then that will point to my take on the situation. I see you found the remote and the bed, and of course, into my apartment without a key."

"You left the door open, and the remote fills up space like a statue of King David. How can you miss it, and how do they know what King David looked like?"

"I never leave the door open, and I know you're going to stick with that story."

"The door was open."

"Okay, let me check the news channels." He pushes one button on the remote, turning on the news.

I'm thinking, *A picture within a picture, behind a picture, those without eyes may not recognize.* "What?"

Apparently, I'm talking out loud again instead of thinking.

I explain, "These are words to a George Clinton song. It's just something I say to myself when I'm trying to read between the lines. At least I think those are the words. You know when what you're singing goes along with the beat, so you go with it."

The news is playing in the background and nothing so far about the shooting at the club. I ask about the chessboard and if he knows how to play or if is it just for show.

"Yeah, I play a little, but you know that already. You know, since that bump on the head, you've been acting strange. It seems like you remember when it matters, I guess in order of importance."

I'm thinking he knows a little more about a lot of stuff, or I haven't asked the right question. I'm wondering if I told him that I am working on a new way to play the game of chess.

Cleo breaks into my conversation with myself. "You did say, remember? You said the pieces would be the same but some of the movements would be changed and the board would be extended. Of course, I'm still trying to master the original way, you know, the way the whole world has been playing for thousands of years."

"You sound like Dewayne; he told me the same thing."

He agrees. "Dewayne's a very good player."

I tell him I know. He also asks why would I want to change the game that's been played this same way for thousands of years. He seems emotional about it. He goes on to say something about strategies and that one would have to be a genius to do that. I tell him I am. I don't think he believes me. I tell him I have talked to some young chess champs, and they say why not, so I'm going for it. Just like we have new ways to fight wars, why not change the oldest war game? I have a plan.

He encourages me with agreement. "Right, a plan is the best start for any kind of success. Look, there is nothing on the news about the shooting, which means, the powers that be are at work on their plan. It's a simple thing called a sweep, in the business."

"Meaning what?"

"Well, they get rid of anyone that may be close enough to us, where we may tell any details or put two and two together about a job."

"River, and Joy; I need a phone."

"Relax, River's too young and you said your mother suggested you call Joy. Hopefully, she made this suggestion over the phone, where they'll have a recording of you still calling just to check in on them. I wouldn't go into a lot of who, what, when, where, how, about too much of anything at this point. You see, normally they sweep after the job. This must be big."

In a low, concerning voice I ask about the other people in the room. "What about Flo and Open Mic; I saw O.M. take one to the chest on his life-sized poster. When I got outside, there were no signs of him or you. I jumped over bodies on the floor as I was getting out of the club."

"He may have been wearing a vest, anyway."

"A vest?"

"You know, bulletproof, Kevlar."

"Okay, but why?"

He explains something I should know already.

"Sometimes spoken Word art rubs the crazy people in the world the wrong way."

"What is he, besides the spoken word?"

"Don't know, don't want to know. The less you know about a lot of stuff the better. I'm guessing you still remember enough but not too much, or you'd be dead. I'll remind you of the stuff that matters. I got your back my friend! I know a little about a lot of stuff. I just look like this."

I still need to talk to my little girl. I have to put my hands on a phone. "Hello, may I speak to River?"

Joy knows me from my voice, and I imagine her smiling, "Okay, just a minute. River, it's your dad."

"Daddy! I miss you! Where are you?"

"I'm at Mr. Cleo's place. Have you been good?"

"Yes."

"That's my girl. What about schoolwork?"

"It's good, Ms. Joy helps me do it, and she says if I do well in school, she has a surprise for me."

"Do you need a surprise to do well in school?"

In a low voice, she says, "No, I'll do well no matter what, but I do like surprises."

"I know you do. Let me speak to Mommy, I mean, Ms. Joy."

"How is Mommy? I miss her, too. Where is she? Can I talk to her? When can I see her?"

"She's okay. Can I talk to you later about Mommy?"

River calls out to Joy with an interesting choice of words. "Ms. Joy, my daddy needs you."

"Coming. I'm sorry, I was listening. You haven't told her?"

"I don't know how."

"I know it's not easy, but it will get better."

"You seem sure, considering what you've been through. Does time heal all wounds?"

"There's only one way from down and that's up," Joy replies.

"Or further down and then out."

"Don't talk like that. Life and death are in the power of the tongue, so speak life. Are you going to be okay?" she ask as if she could tell I was dealing with more today than before. I know she just wants me to stay positive.

"I'm not too bad, just checking in on you two. What is this surprise River speaks of?"

"Just a little something. Are you coming over? I'll surprise you, too."

"Yes, but not now, soon."

"Okay, be thankful and be careful."

"You, too."

It's a relief to hear their happy voices. I have so many questions—how, what, when, where, and why—never in the same order every day now.

"Have you heard from Flo?" I ask Cleo.

"She may not have made it, and I'll have to be okay with it, but we'll know soon enough. I think she is cool with who I am showing her right now, instead of what I could be. Maybe she sees what she could change me into. It seems like she's happy with herself because she's a singer and delivers the spoken word. She has an opinion about most things. The downside to that quality is she could be considered a threat when she speaks truth to power. What you do, where you live, the shows you watch on TV, is it FOX News, CNN or do you See Bull S[]#t; sorry I mean CBS, your hobbies, the movies you rent, the food you buy on your card, your education levels, down to your friends, gives the powers that be a profile of you, and they act accordingly. Everyone has a level of threat, from very high to low. They could see a threat in her and if so, just because I met her, she did not make it through the night."

"What about O.M.?"

"I've known O.M. about the same time I've known you. He has the same story as me and others depending on the moment in time, as we know it. Your wife is dead, as is his wife, at least dead to him, they don't communicate. He has a twenty-six-year-old son who just moved to the West Coast to be with his real mother. I don't recall him saying he ever married his son's mother. He has published work in magazines, and short stories in journal form. There is a copy on the table to the right of you."

Let us see, nice cover. "On Me," the title. The face and eyes move to follow you then fade to white. This cover may have cost a pretty penny. Let us see what's inside.

Introduction: Into the Mind of Open Mic.

I remember the feeling I got when seeing a real brain for the first time, unable to describe it or recall where I was. I know I've never felt the feeling since.

The first thing you need to know about me is I have memories, but I no longer have the pain, or the scar or do I? I barely remember her name. I'm blessed, in short, to tell you how I stay positive. It's God's relationship with me. I, too, worship before the matter at hand and that's what has carried me through and has restored me on the other side.

Real Love

All I felt important was gone now. The beginning of the end was when we lost our child by miscarriage. I was accused of not caring. She couldn't see my pain. I showed little emotion, which is common with men across the board I'm afraid. Somehow, I picked up the notion that I shouldn't show much feeling, you know poker face and don't let them see you sweat. I remember trying to stay strong and encouraging. It was viewed as callous and uncaring. The fact was, I didn't know what to think, say, or do. I felt empty inside. I just lost a baby I was trying to have. I recall saying to myself, was this the pound of flesh needed as payback?

My firstborn in marriage was taken for all the babies aborted outside of Holy wedlock. My soul cries out an apology to each girl who had to kill a baby because boys aren't man enough to be daddies. My God, continue to bless the ones that made it through. I was crushed and to add to that pain the notion of me not caring. Should I buy flowers, and watch them die, too?

No more death I say to myself, I'll buy this carving of an elephant. I was trying to say we'll never forget, as if we could. Think of a branch of the family tree that has been cut away. I felt the symbol was enough and still brought the picture frame for what could have been the image. I cut a picture of a little boy playing one drum out of a magazine. It was again too little too late. I lost her. She said I didn't love her enough. I didn't love her as much as I should have, or the way she wanted it. I suppose she figured making a lot of love meant very much in love. Sad I say, for love is deeper than the physical.

On the other hand, I heard as I was growing up that having sex is all boys think about. As time passes, I learned some ladies think of getting it all the time also. The twist is when in that heated moment comes up, the man hears, don't, and stop, don't stop, and as I stop my advance because no means no, I hear, why did you stop? Twisted I say. People should discuss all parts of a relationship because the little things become big over time.

O.M. pours his heart out onto the paper, and they say men don't have deep feelings. That's good stuff to pass on to whoever picks it up and reads. It seems like all of us go through something at one time or another, I think I'll read a little more.

Letter From Me To You

My Dear,

Hope you're okay; I'm okay. Then sometimes I'm not. I went to call and then all the words I needed to say got folded over themselves. When I'm working, I don't think of us much. There are times when I think of us a lot. The good, the bad, the people that were a part of our circle; I must say, it hurts. My heart hurts over what has happened to us. I apologize and can you forgive me? Forgive me for not loving you enough. I know it's too late for these words to change anything. I wasn't aware I didn't love you in a way you felt loved, and this made you deeply unhappy. You should have said something, and I suppose you feel you did. To hear you say the things you said to me, and with such anger, cut me deep.

It's funny how the body reacts to stress. At that moment my heart broke, and the blood pooled on the surface of my skin, leaving visible scars on my ribs. The doctor said it may never go away. You may think I'm saying these things to make you feel bad, or maybe you feel good over my pain, but I'm not. I just wanted you to know why I could never come back to you. The way you had begun to act, and the words out of your mouth are the reasons I just let us die. I really wanted to fix it at first, if it could be fixed. Then I said how can I stay around someone who could choose to cut me so deep? I'd go mad trying to keep it from happening again. I'd wonder if, and when, and what I would do or say in defense. I hope this letter helps me get over us. Our marriage failed, and it hurts to realize I wasn't enough.

Goodbye

New entry, date unknown.

I look back on this letter and see I ended by admitting to myself the part I played in all that. It was not the quality or the quantity. It was more the little things. So why do we say the little things? Everything is a big deal. Flowers, candy, dinner, dancing, and say I love you, even when I just like you today. I even got therapy about buying dying flowers. I was told to just do it, never mind the waste of hard-earned money. The institution of marriage is just that, an institution. Institutions like good companies need managers, good ones. The time you spend together, mismanaged, will be unproductive. Do you feel me? Maybe the parts that worked were good but not enough, it didn't last. Whatever you label it, it's done.

F—k that;

In all the business of ending our relationship,

I was pissed.

Can you read my pain?

No, you can't.

Words aren't enough.

I can say but unless you walk in this moment, you can't begin to know. It's really worse than heartbreak, because, what God has joined together as one, has become two.

The one body has been torn apart. Picture that. We all become different people when the truth shows itself. As the rain falls and time doesn't heal the wound, we turn cold enough to burn ourselves. Now we lock the pain away inside where it becomes the fuel that ignites thoughts of revenge. Yes, I was mad, and I wanted to fight. How would you feel if you found out some SOB is f————ing your wife? It's bad enough, then you find out it's someone close to your circle of so-called friends. My thought process is when someone you know is stabbing you in the back, it's just plain disrespect. This is the worst thing for me.

I will say, God is great, and timing is everything. It would have been bad for all involved if I had learned of this information before I left and had not seen the promised land, because confrontation would have been unavoidable. I would have needed to have him feel my pain, look me in the eyes to see them cry blood. I'll have to stop here…

Okay, I'm back. I had to let my dogs in. They're outside barking at the demons that have gathered at my window; looking in on the man of God thinking desperately wicked thoughts of how he should deal with the person who took his life. I thank God; an angel is behind me and goes before me. They help hold back sick, twisted restitution. We all are capable of going mad. Most of us never act on our craziness, or insane insanity, which is what we get, when dealing with life outside God's influence. I should say when being disobedient to what we know about God. We cannot act outside God's influence. The enemy will try to kill you with their actions.

Can I stone them to death? Jesus says, He who has no sin throws the first stone. *I'm thinking since Jesus has washed away my sin, where can I find a hill of stones or a brick or two? Okay maybe not till death, but until he felt he was about to die, letting him live in fear of the day when I could come back and do this dance again. I thank God; he had me move before I found out the whole story. My parents are thankful, too. They knew my life still had meaning, and was worth living, hoping I could see it in time. I question all of it at times and never come up with all the answers.*

My friends and family helped me through the times I felt like giving up. I can put these feelings back in the box; it's negative. The power, the heart inside a man without God is desperately wicked, who can know it? The box glows red hot, and it pulls me down like gravity. It's cool, I must say, for it helps me fuel the flame that drives me forward. I know it sounds like hate is my motivation; I hate sin. I suppose it can be my weakness or my strength, in a life fighting failure. From reality to reality, I have a responsibility to the people close to me to keep living.

That was interesting if I say so myself— half-man, half-mad, all Spirit. "Cleo, have you read any of this?"

"A little bit here and there. I figure I'm living it, I don't need to read much more."

Apparently, what I've read and seen is what you're going through," he says. "You may be reading into the mirror. Only in your case, someone has followed through on the twisted working of the heart and mind, in your situation."

"I guess we're like three of a kind," I commented.

"And it's not a bad hand if you're playing poker," Cleo adds. "It's not the best hand, but better than some. "

"Have you spoken to O.M. about what he wrote?" I ask Cleo.

"He said writing is a release from the pain. Writing allows him to see the bigger picture. He's writing down what the voices in his head tell him, so he can see how crazy committing the act would be. Which is good, I told him, keeping all that inside will just eat away at him. He wants to move forward not back. He has enough stress without thinking of taking someone's life, and the consequences that follow, whether you get caught or not. He decided to use his power for good."

I have questions for Cleo. "You had mentioned a bump on the head. What happened, I can't remember?"

He doesn't answer right away. With pause he looks at me, then up at the ceiling. I'm thinking, *is he going to tell me the truth? Why the pause?*

"Well, the short version is you were on the receiving end of a carjacking, after which you bumped your head."

I got time, or do I?"

Cleo goes into detail. "Well, I know people who know people, here is the long version of what I read on the police report. When they walked up on you and asked for your car with a gun pressed to your head, bear in mind, that all this has been pieced together from facts gathered at the crime scene. At some point, you decided not to give up the car and punched the gas pedal. The police figured the bullet didn't go straight through because the car was moving. Seconds later, taking into consideration the tire marks, the car had only moved a few yards, maybe. They figured you stopped once you realized you were hit.

You got out with your registered .9-millimeter and put two rounds into the gunman. He was in critical condition for three weeks before his condition improved. Only God knows why he confessed to the crime. The two of you were found in the street with weapons, and the police had no idea who was doing what or why. He also told police he had help, but decided he would live longer in jail by not saying who was with him.

Cleo continues recounting the account, "The facts pointed to a second person, since your car was missing but found two days later with all the good parts taken off down to the frame and graffiti on the part they lifted behind, ID by Vin#. The police on the street joked about what was lifted out of the report. The gunman mentioned he had a visitor at the hospital. No one believes him because of all the cameras taping all movement in the building. Both of you were under police watch to see who would get well enough to talk to first. Before more of the pieces were put together, it was concluded that what they were looking at was just another shooting out in the street. The camera shows no visitors coming to the gunman's room, but he swears by it. The visitor told him while holding his medication drip line, if he didn't tell the truth about his part in the matter, he would return. Everything in the room was destroyed. And get this, the officer outside the door heard nothing! They found you face down in the street with a 9mm in your hand." I interrupted, "What's up with that? And did you say face down?"

"Yes, I guess you do remember something. Well, the doctor's report states the direction of the bullet was such that it just rolled around the outer edge of the brain. Not much damage considering you got shot in the head. Lucky, blessed, favor, goodness, and mercy following you and all that. It was only a 22-caliber weapon. The projectile traveled through the nasal cavity and down into the roof of the mouth, which is where the doctor removed it. You'll end up like some kind of urban legend, as the story goes, saying you caught the bullet in your teeth. A piece of lead was removed at the entry point. X-rays looked good, specialists were confident they got all the metal fragments.

"So, I got a steel plate in my head? "

"No, believe it or not, they replaced missing bone with bone harvested from stem-cell research."

"Hamburger. So, what about my DNA? Doesn't it have to match the new bone cells, and all that comes with that?"

He responded with a smart remark. "So now I'm a biochemist and yet I have time to moonlight as an overnight package pickup and delivery person."

I replied smartly "You have a lot of information, why not a chemist?"

"Yes, and I only have the information you told me, and you also told me, the doctor said you may experience some memory loss. You don't remember telling me that, or do you?

"I need to lie down."

'Yes, you do that."

"Maybe when I wake up, I'll spend some time with River."

Cleo adds, "And Joy; she sounds like good people, looking after your little girl and all.

"Yes, she is."

"You going to work today?" asks Cleo.

I told him, "No I'm on family leave. Why do you ask?"

"I start my vacation this week, maybe we can make some extra money while we're both off work. Think you're up for that?"

"I guess, I'll let you know when we get closer to that day. You know tomorrow is not promised on this earth."

"Okay my friend, you don't have to tell me now. It's just some small jobs, nothing we can't get out of in case you're not up to it."

"Cool; peace and thanks for looking out," I say.

"Peace. Lock up if you leave, and here's a key."

"What?"

"Nothing, talking to myself."

"You know you can get medication for talking to yourself." As he walks out, I'm thinking, it must have been a serious bump on the head, because I've misplaced a lot of information about myself. It's gone until it's not. How do they grow bones? How do you dig up memories, or do I want to, maybe I forgot for good reason? Around and around with unanswered questions, I sink deeper and deeper into this Lazy-Boy. A visit from the Sandman and I'm out.

CHAPTER 6

Intermission

She is so beautiful, isn't she? Lovely, sitting with her puzzle, without anything puzzling on her mind, not a care in the world, as it should be. Her smooth, light brown skin has yet to develop stress lines or wrinkles. Looking at that Mona Lisa-like smile, I wonder if she is thinking about where her mommy is, why she is going to school from here, and when she will go home to sleep in her own bed. Maybe she wants a different doll. I hope she likes the doll I gave her. I can only pray that one day the Lord will bless me with a strong, healthy, smart child like her. "Ms. Joy, why are you looking at me?"

"I admire your Mona Lisa smile. You're doing so well on your puzzle. I was thinking of asking what you were thinking."

"I'm thinking about Daddy and where is Mommy? Where is she? I haven't heard from her in a long time."

Okay, God, what do I tell her? Well, at least I know what she's thinking, and she's smiling, so I hope that's a good sign. She's not worried yet. What should I say? Okay, she doesn't know the details, and why should she? At least not from me.

"Your daddy says the doctor has to run some tests to help us find out why she's sleeping so much. We will ask your daddy and see if he has any more news about your mommy, okay?

"Okay. Ms. Joy. What's a Mona Lisa smile?"

"Well, the Mona Lisa is the name of a painting made by a very famous artist from the old days. The lady in the painting has a special smile that makes some people wonder what she is thinking. It's like a smile, but some of us aren't really sure."

"I hope she's thinking something good. Do you know the artist's name?"

"Leonardo da Vinci."

River's eyes brighten. "I know him, or maybe not. Did Ninja Turtle Michelangelo paint the Sistine Chapel?"

Joy, with a smile, explains that the turtle and the artist are not the same and only have the same name, complimenting River. "Aren't you the smart one to have an appreciation for art?"

"Yes, thank you."

"Maybe we can go to the museum and see more artwork. Would you like that?"

"Yes, I would, and can we get cookies and ice cream?"

"I think we can do that."

River's head turns toward the sound. "The phone's ringing. I hear it," she says as she runs to the phone. "I'll get it. Ms. Joy's resident. River speaking. Who's calling? Yes. Yes. Ms. Joy, a lady named Bernadette wants to speak to you!"

I answer her with correction. "That would be *Ms.* Bernadette to you, and you can hang up. I have it."

Bernadette answers with a happy greeting. "Hey, girl. It's been a while. How are you doing?"

"I'm doing okay, considering..."

"What?"

"You know my husband had been sick?"

"I know."

"Well, he made his transition into the next life a few weeks ago."

"He died? Oh, baby, I'm sorry to hear that. Can I do anything?"

"No, everything has been taken care of, and I have a little helper. She is good company and God's blessing of a distraction. She answers the phone and keeps my mind off all the stuff that goes with losing a family member."

"Who does that child belong to?"

"She is the offspring of an old friend of mine. I am his first love, in fact, at twelve years old, or however much in love one can be in at twelve going on thirteen."

"You mean from around the corner from Mom's house?" Bernadette's voice has a high pitch now.

"Yes, I told you about him?"

"You did tell me some time ago, long before you were even married."

"Okay, well, his wife was killed a few days ago—"

"What the hell?" Bernadette shrieks. "I mean, I'm sorry. Is he involved in what I've been reading about in the paper? Do you think he did it?"

"No!"

Bernadette goes into a theoretical rant. "I bet you that the police think so, especially after the OJ Simpson trials. For every wife that comes up missing or killed, the police point the finger at the husband no matter where he was when it happened. I hope he has a good alibi."

"I'm sure he does, and yes, they do look at the husband first."

"Did you do it? Well, it has only been a few days since your husband passed and is now out of the way, and the only thing keeping you two apart is his wife, and now you are taking care of his daughter after a mystery killing of his wife. It is not impossible; it just means you had to work fast like you had it all planned once you learned why and how sick your husband was."

"Imagine that, scandalously romantic, and somewhat sick," I say with sarcasm. "I know we haven't talked in a while, but do you want me to hang up on you, or just sign over to you the book and movie rights to that story? Besides, he called me, and it can be seen as a simple home invasion gone wrong at a bad time. The newspaper says, 'It looks like a crime of passion because she was found dead with her lover.'"

Bernadette sucks her teeth. "And the plot thickens."

"You crazy, girl. Well, consider maybe I'm just being considerate and helping myself to a nice change in direction by keeping his little girl."

"I can see that, and also see how blessed a person can be by helping someone else plow through life. I can keep my mess to myself."

Taking the focus off me, I ask, "What's up? Why did you call?"

"It's small compared to what you're going through, but my brother has to go on dialysis."

"Sorry to hear. There's a lot of that going around. River's grandfather is in that situation as well."

"How's he doing?"

I try to give a positive outlook. "It's been about ten years. I guess if you stay on top of it, listen to the doctors, and not try to do the procedures from home, the setbacks can be few."

"But my brother, he's so young; I wish we could have known the signs and avoided this chapter of life. I'll pass this information on to my mom. She's stressing over the whole thing. Thank you for the straight talk."

"Life is short. Not a lot of time left to put sugar on top of a meat issue."

"Since we're talking, don't be around that little girl looking beat down. We see life is trippin', but we don't have to look like it. Keep your nails and your hair did, and take your little helper with you. Everyone will appreciate it, trust me on this one. That's where I'm headed now. I'll be looking good inside my little mess."

I smile. "Okay, I hear you, and nice talking to you."

"I love you, and keep me posted."

"Love you, too."

CHAPTER 7

Me

My calls go straight to voicemail. I hope everything is okay. I'll just head over. It seems like I haven't seen River in weeks, but it's only been a few days. If they're not home, I'll stop by the job and pick up my check stub just to get some air. The money is already in the bank, direct deposit. Cleo has a nice place, but it's not home.

Nice area... I hope I've followed the directions correctly. Let's see, looking for Deer Run—Street, Road, Avenue, End? That's funny. Okay, my friend, pick one since you have no cell phone service up here. Let's try Deer Run Road. Nice place. I guess I'll offer to cut the grass while I'm here if this is the right house. Good guess—the name is on the bell, but no one's home. Right, I'll leave a note and come back later.

Plan B: pick up my check stub. Bill Withers' "A Lovely Day"—I wouldn't mind hearing that CD right now. Do I have it with me? Yes, I do. Unspeakable joy.

I'm at the work site now, and this should be interesting. Jay greets me, as I walk onto the parking lot.

"Check out what the weather blew in. What's up, man? You clocking in today?"

"No, I'm just out getting some air and picking up my check stub."

Jay is always in help mode. "You should have called; you know I would have put that in the mail for you."

"I know, my union dues dollars at work, but my house is still a crime scene complete with yellow tape. I'm not trying to relive all that just to make sure they got my paycheck correct. I'll have to go into the community to get to the mailboxes and pass the place where it happened. I see it played back while I drive down the street, so being on location will prove to be a bit much. It's better if I stay away. I'll most likely pull a Michael Jackson and just sell the place without ever going back, you know, like Neverland. I'm trying to let the scar heal."

"I can understand. Hope I never have to go through something like that, and I'm sorry you have to deal with it."

Jay is the union shop steward for this location and works on the afternoon shift. I wouldn't want his responsibility, everybody coming to him with how they get caught doing something they should not have been doing, in most cases.

Jay tries to gain some information, and it's okay, part of the job, I guess. "Frankly, the fellows are trying to piece together what's up with you. You ran out of here yesterday like O.J. without the white Bronco chasing you down the street. Can you tell me anything more than what we read in the paper or see on the news?"

"Not really, but I can say the police have found out who the headless man was in my bedroom, but they still haven't found his head.

"*Damn,* no matter how many times I hear headless, it just kicks me back. That's crazy. Movies are one thing, real life is something else."

I can tell he isn't trying to be nosey, his face tells the story, with one raised eyebrow, a twisted corner of his mouth, and him just trying to process the situation. His expression changes as he moves on to another subject.

Jay now shares the latest madness at the job. "Did you hear about what was found written on the restroom wall here at work?

"No, what?"

"It doesn't stack up to what you're going through, but the madness is still the same. Someone wrote their opinion about the immigration policy we have here in America. I get mad when I think about it for too long. I drew a picture on a piece of paper of what I saw."

He hands me a blank grievance form so I can make my complaint about what he told me, as if he knows I will have something to say and wants it for the record. We walk to the restroom, and he shows me the wall. I think it's sad because this kind of behavior makes for a hostile work environment. How do I process the person next to me? Can they be wishing I would drop dead?

Most people can listen to a racial joke and not get offended. I guess it depends on the setting. Comments like, "Go back to your motherland, niggers," and "Learn the language, Mexican mf," or "WHITE POWER," complete with Nazi stickers. While I take all this in, I can only shake my head.

Jay comments, "Deep, right?"

"Somebody's trippin' hard. Why is it still on the wall?"

"Supervisors are going to paint over it after taking pictures. They had good intentions, but the photos will come out too small to do handwriting comparisons. Other parts of the bathroom with writing on the wall will also have to be painted, so they will use those writings to investigate. Authorities will be using paperwork that is already on file. Stuff like applications, and vehicle inspection logbooks, you know, the paper we write on every day. They will prosecute if they can pin someone down for the act. I guess if you really hate me, sooner or later, I'll find out."

"You know six boys are on trial for conspiracy to commit murder because they sat together at lunch and talked about having a white's only seating area discontinued. The area is under a large oak tree on the school grounds, a public school. A fight broke out and the boys were charged, and one white person who was found not to be a student was also charged with trespassing. The Black students are facing ninety-nine years, for they were heard talking about the tree, so it was said that they planned the fight. One of the boys is already in jail and sentenced to twenty-two years for the alleged conspiracy."

"The Justice System is still unfair in 2007."

"And the beat goes on. And on that note, I'm out. Talk to you soon."

As I make my way from the parking lot to the office, the distance feels longer than usual. The way the guys are looking at me, it makes me wonder what's going through their minds. Some of them acknowledge me with a greeting, while others remain silent. Maybe it's just my imagination, but I can't shake off the feeling that they might be judging me.

I can't help but think about the news they must have seen or read. They must be aware of the disturbing details surrounding the alleged killer who works alongside us. It's unsettling to realize that I once gave him a ride home when his car broke down. We drove for sixty-five miles together, and now it dawns on me that he could have done something unthinkable during that time. It's a harsh reminder that no matter how well you think you know someone, there's always a chance of being deceived.

The people in the office are polite; I can hear them talking, and it's mighty big of me to think it's about me. My supervisor asks when I think I'm coming back to work; I answer him with some humor, saying, "If my paycheck is correct, I'll come back to work the day after tomorrow." He just looks at me with no expression because I'm sure that's not the answer he's looking for. On top of that, he's probably thinking to himself that if I am serious, there's a good chance I won't be back anytime soon because our paychecks have about a thirty-five percent chance of being wrong.

I'm going through a box where they keep the checks, and there's a silent drum roll in my head. The people in the office are waiting to see if my check is going to be right, and whose life I'm going to take if it's not. Yes, that's right, they don't know if I'm a killer or not. Or is someone really doing a drum roll and I think it's all in my head?

I tear open the envelope and it seems like the whole office is at a standstill, and yes, it's wrong. I give the correction to the clerk in charge of payroll, and I walk out. Looking over my shoulder, I see my supervisor walking back to his office with his head bowed because he will have to figure out who will do my route again. Even though it's overtime when someone has to do my route, it's forced overtime, and most of the drivers have enough to do on their own routes.

They've been working since 7:00 a.m. After doing my route, it's now 11:00 p.m. and still hot, like eighty-six degrees, and they have to be back by 7:00 a.m.

I'll get back to work as soon as I can because I hate being forced to work past my regular time. Do unto others as you would have them do unto you. I guess that it will be some time before I'll have to do overtime; being on trial for murder has a curfew.

Now I'm on my way to the parking lot and I see Cleo, who is supposed to be on vacation.

"Cleo, what's up man? I thought you were on vacation."

"I am, but they called to see if I would come in, so I said yes. I was bored anyway, and work isn't as bad when you don't have to do it, but as life goes, once I said I was coming in, I got a call to put in some work. They gave up some more details, so I need to check it out. What are you about to do?"

"I'm giving River and Joy a call, hoping to go by there on my way back to your apartment."

"That's cool. I'll call you when I'm done here. Maybe we can make this run together if you're up to it."

"Yes, as long as you're driving."

"I can do that."

"If I'm done at Joy's place, I can go with you. Peace."

"Peace."

I head to my car, searching for my cell. It is not in this pocket and not in the other one either. Where is it? I don't have my phone. How did that happen? Okay, it's one of those days; back inside.

Office agent says, "You're back!"

"I need to use the phone, is that okay?"

"You can use the one in the break room."

Still, no one is home. Maybe I'll sit in my car under a tree for a minute and give them time to make it back to the house. It is a nice day, not too hot today, and a good breeze to go with this perfect day. The downside is that the wife was murdered while committing adultery.

In most circumstances, the last thing on most people's minds is, when will the insurance company pay out? Since she's turned out to be a lying cheat, I want what's mine, and I'll move on. My guess is this won't happen until after the investigation. My soul searches for peace in all these moments of unspeakable joy. I haven't been to church or spoken to my pastor about any of this. I could hear his voice quoting scripture, "Count it all joy."

The sound of moving cars, trucks, and doors closing hard fills the air. I recall my last working day and having an air-conditioned van. At the end of the day, I put a chain on the steering wheel, hoping to get that van the next day. I didn't lock the van down, but it made the van appear out of service to anyone who looked in the window.

The vans with air conditioning are few, so all I'm trying to do is ensure I have a good day tomorrow. I want to think it wouldn't have been so bad if I hadn't given my two cents to another driver about coming to work early to get keys to vans with air conditioning and how he shouldn't do that. It could have been seen as trespassing or stealing since this driver wasn't on the clock yet. The union frowned upon people doing that, but since there was no enforcement of the rules from the office, drivers continued to work off the clock. I'm in that gray area when I'm on the clock, putting the mechanic's out-of-service chain on the wheel. My justification is the hope that he will not get keys to a van that appears out of service. I say, all in a day's work. I'm the pot calling the kettle black. It's a good day to witness the madness. The time it takes to live a life feels like forever. The time it takes to get it right spills into a second lifetime. Writing about it will take the rest of your life.

I guess I'll get back to Cleo's and stop by Joy's on the way. I have a cup of coffee first, and I pull up too close again; now my bumper is hooked on the curb. I pull back slowly, and yes, my bumper is hanging off now, just as I picture the sound it makes. Don't panic. Let's see if it will pop back in the same way it pops out. Yes, it does. Not perfect, but not hanging. I need to stop drinking coffee or use the drive-thru whenever I can.

I order one small iced coffee, no cream, no sugar. I roll up to Joy's house; her car is out front, a good sign. I knock on the door and hear footsteps.

Joy greets me with a smile. "A good day to you."

"A good day to you, too."

"What a nice surprise."

I tell her surprise isn't the goal and that I've been calling, but no one answered.

Joy explains they were out shopping and had closed down the museum.

I say, "Okay." She goes on to say my daughter wants to see the Mona Lisa. " Did my little get to see it?"

"No, not the real one, but they had some nice lithographs for sale." She smiles and looks over her shoulder. "River, your daddy is here."

River sees me and runs into my arms. "Daddy, Daddy, Daddy!"

I'm happy she's happy to see me. "My sweetest of hearts, how are you doing?"

"I'm okay," River says with a big smile.

"Just okay, or a little better than okay?"

"Better than okay."

"I thought so."

"Where is Mommy?"

I look over at Joy, wondering how many times she has had to dodge that question with some version of the truth. Joy shrugs and remains silent. I'm thinking, tell some small truth, and only answer what she asks me. So, I tell her the doctors are trying to see why she's so sleepy.

There is a question on her face. "Is she going to be all right?"

"The doctors are looking at her, so let's hope for the best and remember that God is able to make her all better."

Joy jumps in. "Are you going to stay awhile?"

"Yes, but Cleo and I have to make a run to the city later. He said he will call around the time he is ready."

"We were about to have some turkey sandwiches. Would you like one?"

"No, but thank you. It will make me sleepy, and I need to be awake for later."

"That's right. Okay, what about chicken?"

"Chicken's good with some mustard on it please."

"I can do that, and what about some barbecue chips?"

I answer smartly, "Do they make other flavor chips?"

Some time goes by while Joy prepares food. River and I talk about school, and I steer us away from Mommy subjects. Joy comes in with the food and sits down quietly, allowing River and I to talk. Now we're eating, not a lot of words between us, just smiling faces. At this point, I realize I'm hungrier than I thought. I look at River, and she seems happy, as she should be without knowing. She'll have plenty of time to worry or decide to pray about it. I know she thinks about her mom, and I wonder at what age I should let her process this information. I have to wait a little while because she's too young to go into the courtroom with me. I hope

Joy will be okay with keeping River for a little longer. So far, she seems all right with the arrangement. Knowing her story, nothing surprises me anymore. She tells me that each time she goes into detail about what happened to her, people say she should write a book about it and how it could help someone avoid a fatal attraction or encourage someone who's walking in those shoes.

Joy breaks the silence. "How is your chicken?"

"It's good," I reply with my mouth full. "I guess I was hungrier than I thought."

"What about you, River, is your sandwich okay?"

"Yes! And now it's time for *cookies!*"

I look at Joy and then at River. "How many cookies have you had today?"

River looks at Joy and then at me. "No cookies. We had ice cream a long time ago, hours."

She knows timing between snacks is important.

"Okay, some cookies will be all right."

River goes for the gold. "How many, five?"

Now the negotiation starts. "No three."

"Okay, four?"

"No, two."

"How about three?"

"Okay three."

"I'll have cookies please, thank you," River says with a happy dance.

CHAPTER 8

Red and Yellow Kiss a Fellow

Joy wants to make a night of it. "Is anybody up for a game of chance?"

"What kind?" River wants to know.

"Trouble."

I haven't seen that game in a while. "Is that the game where you have a color you must count around the path with the throw of the dice, and when you have all your colors on the same home base first, I win?"

Joy twists her lips while looking out the corner of her eye. "I like the way you put the 'I win' part in there and yes, that is the game."River agrees. "Sounds like fun."

"Let's play," we say in unison.

Joy goes into another room to get the game. River sits with anticipation, and Joy comes back into the room with the box. This is how the game goes. I pick green as the first of the four colors, but there's a protest, so I let them pick ahead of me. River picks yellow, and since there are four choices, I let her pick again. She picks red. Joy knows I want green, so she picks green to throw me off my game. I get the only color left, blue. River goes first, I go last, and Joy is in the middle.

River is ready. "Let's play."

I change the rules a bit to let Joy go first since we are guests in her home. River isn't happy with the new order, so I explain that it's only fair for Joy to go first because River has two colors and a better chance to win.

"Okay," she said.

We are all set to play, and each of us starts the game strong. Joy's first roll is a six. My first thoughts are about her suggesting the game, choosing it, and having the home court advantage. She may do well. Then, to my surprise, River rolls a six too, and so do I. No one is left behind. River has two colors to move around the board, and it's no surprise she rolls another six. The game starts with four sixes, and my mind wanders to what I've heard about numbers in the Bible. The number six means work, but I'm not sure what four means. I'll have to find out. Joy informs me that four means testing. I guess I was talking out loud again instead of thinking.

We eat, we play, and we laugh out loud when someone has to start over if they land on top of someone else's pieces. It seems like a short time, but hours pass. River wins; the odds and the roll of the die are in her favor, and that's the story I'm sticking to.

I hear someone's phone ringing. I can't find mine. I thought I had it earlier today.

Joy says, "Not my tone." Sounds like mine, but where is it coming from? Okay, I guess I do have my phone. Joy chuckles. "It's the size of a credit card, no wonder you have a hard time finding it."

"It's Cleo, said he might call, I need to take this."

"You think you're up to make this run?" Cleo ask.

"Where?"

"To the city." I pause and then said, "I hate going to the city."

"I'll drive."

"Okay, I'm in." Cleo instructs me to meet at the spot.

"Okay, see you in a minute or two." I explain to them that I have to leave even though we are having a good time. River isn't happy about it and asks me not to go. It's hard listening to her request and looking at her face. "Don't go, Daddy."

"I'm sorry, I promised a friend I would help him in the city, not to mention, it's time for you to get ready for bed. I'll see you in a few days."

"Three or four days?" she asks. Her question is with concern and not the happy face I am looking for.

"Can't get much past you. I'll see you in a couple of days, is that better?"

"Yes, two days, not three, right?"

"Right, and I want to thank you, too, Joy for the food and game."

"You are welcome, it has been no problem at all."I can see a warm smile and bright eyes, not sad that I had to leave, but happy that I was able to sit and visit for a while. Not to mention the hugs and kisses, putting smiles on everyone's faces.

CHAPTER 9

Game Over

The club has a nice vibe tonight. The looks are good all around, welcome to the Double Dutch—no matter who's turning you can always jump in.

The bartender sees me walking toward the bar. "What's up, money? What're you having?"

"Mountaineer, please."

"Coming right up."

No minutes pass and Cleo walks in.

"What's up, money?"

"Chilling, waiting."

The bartender greets Cleo. "My man, what's it gonna be?"

"Apple Martini without the funny glass."

"Coming right up."

I watch him drink it down. "Those things are going to give you high blood pressure."

"I know you're right, and this is my last one," he answers with a straight face.

"Oh, just like that."

"Yes."

He has a serious look on his face as if he's telling the truth, so I agree with him, saying, "Me, too!" I'm considering changing the subject to the details of the job, and I'm also thinking about all the people in the club who could overhear our conversation. I figure we'll have plenty of time to talk in the car on the way into the city, with fewer ears around. We sit for a minute to take in some of the show. The thin red veil comes down, so most of the regular customers know Open Mic is up next on stage.

There he sits with the guitar he never plays. I'm hearing only bits and pieces of the show as I'm looking at all the pretty faces. I hear him say money, and I focus. He's talking about money and the lack of it, or the more of it you have is equal to the level of pain received to make it.

"You know the cost we pay to be able to buy, and if you are willing to pay, is that all you're living for. This is such a waste of life; to want to wear those gold chains of debt. Break that chain and free the life that remains. Pay your dues in a higher and greater calling with less pain. The tears of joy that express having

the debt paid, and passing down to your children the way to be made free of a debt they could not pay, and then put forth the efforts which affect the reward gained from the gift that will never wither away. All depends on the work put forth before you, and now it's your turn. I'm about done. Even then life has no guarantee, but tomorrow is. It's only in death that we receive what's promised, everlasting life, but where?"

Fingers popping and the stage lights fade to black.

"Let's go before the next show."

"I'm with you," I answer as I finish my drink.

Some time goes by, a little over a mile a minute, and we don't speak on the details of the job. There is a long wait at the tunnel and then I see skyscrapers and everything, trash, broken bottles, rats, roaches, junkies laying right in the street, homeless people without enough to eat, pickpockets, and panhandlers. The big city hasn't changed much since my last visit.

Cleo makes a few more turns and we are at what they call The Business Center of the World. We park with surprising ease, it's late, so there are no meters to feed. We walk through the glass doors, me first, down some stairs then onto escalators. All stores are closed. The cleaning crews are walking around. I am doing some window shopping. Cleo is making notes and drawing sketches, and no one seems to be paying us any attention. I get the feeling they're with us.

I see a great-looking watch. I want it, but the shop seems closed. The lights are on inside, but not in the display case. Cleo is walking ahead of me, taking notes, and maybe hasn't noticed I stopped. It's a nice watch; not too flashy, with four rectangular diamonds about two carats each. It's like a new classic, with two hands showing the time and a digital display on the side counting backwards to May 11, 2011. Harold Campy said that the date would be the end of days as we know it.

I grab the doorknob to the store and imagine that, it was open. At this hour maybe the owner is catching up on some paperwork in the back and forgot to lock the front door. I have a nice watch now, but the one on display is nicer. You know it seems like it's never enough.

By now, Cleo is doubling back and walking past the window as I reach the display case. He looks me square in the face, then both ways. I grab the watch and leave. The door closes behind me, and there's no alarm unless it's silent. We are about thirty feet from the store, and no security is in sight.

Seeing the disappointment on his face, he shakes his head. "You risk everything for a gold watch that has diamond markers for numbers, and you only get one. You're thinking kind of small right now and when this job goes down, you'll be able to buy a watch twice as nice."

You know what seems funny to me is how he doesn't see what we were doing by stealing; it's more like a redistribution of wealth.

It is at that moment we hear four deafening explosions, each one echoing through the air with a deep, resounding thud.

"What was that?" Cleo reaches for his gun.

"I don't know."

Cleo breaks out running, and I am right behind him. He knows where we are in the building, but I don't. The floor and walls shake from the blast and start to crumble. Glass shatters from most of the stores, and there's the sound of bending steel beams. If you can't imagine that, think of the sound of a creaking door, but much louder, with added vibrations. Now alarms, bells, whistles, and flashing red lights are all going off in unison. The cleaning crews and a few security personnel are all running towards exit signs and stairs, as are we. Up one, two, three flights—*How far down are we?*

We run down the hall to reach another door and up a final flight of stairs, hoping to get out onto the streets. Most of the main power in the building is out. I can barely see through the dust and water from busted pipes and crumbling concrete walls. I can almost see Cleo at the exit door. He pushes on the door, but it won't open. I am five steps away when the lights go out completely, pitch black; no flashing emergency red sirens, bells, or horns. All I can hear is a loud silence and the sound of Cleo pushing at the exit door. I don't miss a step and run blindly toward the sound. When I reach him, we push together through the door and fall straight down.

I assumed the platform was there leading outside or to more stairs, but it wasn't. Now the emergency power on the busted glass on the exit sign was in operation. It was difficult to see through all the falling debris, floating dust, and water. I can see broken steam pipes and downed electrical wires had presented a special dread, while I tried to focus my eyes on the glow from the exit sign. There was no clearing or space unhampered by broken pieces of concrete and twisted metal.

I don't want to wipe my eyes for fear of making a bad situation worse, like trying to get dead bugs off the windshield with wipers but no fluid. I open, close, then open my eyes again, trying to stay focused on the light. Hope is necessary. I hope it's the same exit sign from the door we fell from and not two or three levels down. That's not a good thought; let's stay positive and focus on what we want, not what we don't want. We need to get out of here.

It was getting hard to breathe now, so I needed to see if I can move. My legs seemed okay; my feet checked to my toes with no pain. I tried to stand up, and "Ahh, that hurts!" I feel pressure at my waist, and now the blood, and all kinds of pain. Out of sight, out of mind in its truest form, I didn't feel it until I tried to use it. I wondered if I can outthink and not see the piece of metal going right through my newly acquired watch and my waist. Just another thing I was not sure of. Like, how deep into my waist does this piece of metal go? It was bleeding pretty badly. It was decision time. Do I keep the piece of metal in the watch or take it off and risk more pain and bleeding, or how close am I to the major artery in that area? It would be a good time to use my powers for my own good.

I hear my phone, but where is it? Keep ringing, ring, ring. Now leave a message, and I will have one more chance to hear if they leave a message. *Oh God, please have someone call me, please, please call me. Thank you, God. I can hear it, and I can see it. Can I reach it? My arm is wet now, with lots of blood, and it feels cold and numb. Move, you can do it. I've got you.*

"Hello, hello?"

"What's up? Can you hear me?"

"Barely, now I can."

I hear the sound of cars, horns, and sirens—sounds like Cleo made it out. But how?

So, I ask, "Where are you?"

"Turn around, I'm behind you."

Again, with the horn, and it's louder now. I open my eyes, sit up, and turn around, only to realize I'm in my car. Cleo has gotten off work and is calling me to see if I can make that run with him. He saw my car in the parking lot, surprised that it is still parked from earlier today. He pulls up alongside me, but not directly next to me. I still have to use the side mirror to see his car. When I don't move, he gets out and looks down into my window.

Cleo laughs. "Wake up, man. How are you still here?"

"I guess I drifted off. I called Joy and River to see if I could come by, but they weren't home. I was thinking I would just chill here for a minute and give them time to get home instead of going back to the apartment.

"I had a crazy dream about a building falling in on me and you after a series of explosions. Joy and River were there also, but not in the building. I did visit them in the dream. I guess then you called and asked me to meet you at the club, then we took your car to the city. I need to catch my breath."

He looks at me strangely. "Really heard bombs going off, it was hard to breathe at times? Well, let's analyze all that. There could be a good reason for all that besides what you ate before falling asleep. The loud bomb-like noises could have come from people closing truck doors here in the parking lot. You say you were having difficulty breathing; this may have been from exhaust pipes, especially if a truck was parked here beside you for any period of time. As for Joy and River, well I'll leave that insight up to you, and me, okay, you're not my type."

I think for a minute. "You make good points, and I know the brain is funny that way."

Cleo says, "Now that we have all that out of the way, can you make this run downtown with me?

"Let me guess, the Twin Towers."

"Yes, how do you know?"

"That was the building in my dream."

"Okay, now I'm trippin'"

"Let me check on River and Joy. I told them I would try to see them today. I'll just confirm for tomorrow. It wouldn't be fair for River to be up at that late hour, she should be asleep. I wouldn't want to go by late and just see Joy. I don't want to send the wrong message," I say, talking out loud to myself.

He just stands there shaking his head, with one eyebrow raised. "You don't have to explain to me."

"I'm going to take off my work uniform and put on the Gorilla wear gear."

"Why are we expecting bullets in the air today?"

"You can never know at this point, and having bulletproof garments can't hurt. I'm not walking around with the words: BULLETPROOF across my chest just garments that are bullet proof."

"Do we need tools?"

"Most likely not, I'm just going to take some notes as I look around. Listen to you. Do we need tools? You don't use tools when you have 'em."

"I'm good with what I have. I'm going to get something to eat; I'll meet you at your place."

"Bet, that sounds like a plan."

CHAPTER 10

Real Talk

The phone rings a few times, and as I'm thinking of the message I will leave, Joy picks up.

"Good evening."

"Hello, how are you doing?"

Joy sounds happy to hear it's me. "It's you. Hi, sugar, hold the phone. I'm talking to my brother. I'll be right back. Can you hold?"

"Okay."

The greeting she gives makes me feel good. Maybe she won't take it the wrong way if I tell her she and River were in a dream I had. I've been missing River, and Joy has been my friend for a long time. *I might be missing affection*, I say to myself, or at least I think I'm just thinking. Apparently, I've been talking out loud. Joy chimes right in on the conversation with me.

"I miss affection, too. I know River misses you, she told me so. Are you coming over? I'm sorry, was that forward?"

"I guess maybe forward to someone you don't know. At best I don't have to ask what you're thinking or feeling. Your enthusiasm makes it hard to answer your question, and now I'm feeling apologetic, but no. I was calling to see if tomorrow is a good day to spend time with the two of you."

Joy doesn't seem to be disappointed and answers right away. "Yes, I normally have River home by four, so five would be good."

"Okay, good time for me, too.

"I have a surprise for you."

"I'm sure this is the second time you've mentioned a surprise. Can I get a hint this time?"

"Okay, you'll have to take a ride, that's your hint."

I offer my help since I am on my way to the city. "I'm going to the city with Cleo. Maybe if it's a gift, that's wrapped I can pick it up for you, save some gas."

"No, what I got for you doesn't have to come from the city."

"Okay, so you just gonna leave a brother guessing."

"Yes, and see you tomorrow, bye."

"Bye."

I can 'see' her smiling through the phone.

After some Popeye's chicken, I find myself in front of Cleo's place just as he is walking out. I open my door and get out of the car.

"Whose car are we taking?" I ask.

"Yours since you're right here, mine is out back."

At that moment we both see a bright light.

I turn away. "What was that?"

I don't know what that is. Cleo has questions, and it seems like he might have an idea.

"What time is it?"

I try to lighten the tension with my response. "What time is it right now or as opposed to the end of life as we know it?"

Cleo has left his watch inside and says, "I don't know about the end of life as we know it, as you put it."

"It will start to end on May 21, 2011; at least as I figure counting what's left on the clock you have on the wall in the apartment."

"It's a novelty gift. I haven't given much thought to the actual day it is counting down to. You have a watch; what time is it?"

"Nine thirty-one p.m. eastern or we have three years, ten months, twenty-five days, eight hours., seven minutes, forty-six seconds till the end of life as we know. The eyes of big brother watching us all, at least watching the people left behind after the second coming of Jesus."

"Your watch says all that?"

"Yes, I can also break it down to just count the months left, days, hours, or whatever."

The bright light disappears without a trace or source. I notice other people in cars and walking in the street looking at me, watching them as if I have an answer. I do not.

Before I can ask what again, Cleo says, "That was different. Let's turn on the radio. Maybe someone else saw and called in a report."

We ride out into the city, listening to music, waiting for the DJ to break in with a "this just in," but nothing happens. I'm not surprised no one called in to report; we didn't. What do I say to explain what we saw without sounding crazy? I guess no harm, no foul—at least nothing foul that I can see.

The Twin Towers are in sight, with bright lights, skyscrapers, and everything just like I pictured it. I know I say that a lot. I can hear all the sounds of the city; cars and buses zooming by with horns telling us to move out of their way.

I can tell he is thinking about something. "What time is it again 'til the end of time?"

"Three years, ten months, twenty-four days, five hours. Why do you ask?"

"Just checking." He continues. "You dream first, then suddenly the sun shines, and then back to dark. I'm hoping we haven't been thrown around in time for some reason, and you have yet to see the favor God has placed in your life.

Okay, well you can start over in a new life as soon as we tie up the loose ends in your present one."

My brows furrow. "What do you mean favor? What about my wife, my child? Do I even think the unthinkable, my life? She's gone and I'm looking at the circumstances that brought about this chain of events, and as for the doors that opened to me, they were left open."

"Okay, so all the doors were left open, and now you're also the luckiest person I know. I believe some problems are solved by living in the situation. In other words, just keep on living. There are times when we can't explain the obvious because it seems so unbelievable. Look around and pick a number from one to five."

"Okay three."

"I pick two. Okay, that equals five or we can use the number you picked, makes no difference.

"Okay, what are you getting at, Cleo?"

"Work with me."

"Okay then, four."

"Okay, you changed your number, even better. We are going to walk down this street and the fourth door we come to, and the store or building is closed, I want you to push, pull, or grab, and open it."

"Now you trippin."

"I'm tired of this game we live in, and I want out, and I want to be wealthy when I do it. I got a plan that could make us both wealthy. First, I need to know if you're with me. Second, I need to know if you're lucky, blessed, gifted, or good at what you do. All the above works for me. I need you to see that I see you.

"Are you going to tell me this plan?"

"Of course, for the second time, it has a catch. There's good news and bad news; which one do you want first?"

"Bad news first."

"This job is enough to take us out of the game."

"What's the good news?"

"Once I tell you what we can do, you are responsible for the facts you know. The only way to live is to say yes. When you say no, well, you say no to the whole plan, and when the powers that be find out, you become a loose end, and you know what they do with loose ends. Since the MAN knows I brought you in, they'll ask me to take care of it. I'm going to start or end this part of our conversation by saying the role you already play has made you rich and I must tell you that you are already on the hook for being rich. Now, if I tell you what I need to do inside of that, we are in this together all the way, and then we are out for good. You know, after we change our names, location, and some plastic surgery, maybe walk with a limp when you're in public, you know, the price you pay for being a billionaire from someone else's money. Are you ready for this?"

"What, run from the man forever?"

"Yes, and If we do it right, they won't really be sure we did it because everybody disappears, anyway."

"What's the plan, and how much are we talking about?"

"Nineteen billion."

"Nineteen billion, like with a B?"

"Yes, with a B, this is the fourth door; can you open it, or as you put it. Did they leave it open?"

"Yes, it's open; I guess they left it open."

"Try the next door. Was it left open, too?"

"Yes, it's open also. There could be a logical explanation for this coincidence. The two people that were in charge of locking the doors came out together and got side-tracked, talking about catching a cab or movie after dinner, right?"

"Right and the odds of anything happening are greater for nothing happening at all. Yes, two merchants next door to each other leave their stores unlocked and unattended in the middle of the city. Who would think of such a thing besides you? At least we've established what you are working with, and it works well. From the way you answer, I think you believe these doors were left open, and as such, favor is in the strength of your faith. I'll try one. Right, you guessed it, locked solid with a keypad entry system. You try."

"It's open, you must have pushed the right buttons but didn't turn the knob hard enough. You know all these doors could be open. We walk the streets late at night and assume the doors are locked. How many of us don't try believing we were locked out?"

I have no real reason, and my speech turns into a blank look on his face. He seems to accept that for the time being. I have a real reason to consider this line of thinking. We start walking again, and he begins detailing his plan. *It seems simple enough on paper*, as they say.

He starts with the part of the plan I am least likely to agree with. He says we would need two, three, or four dead bodies. I try to maintain a poker face as I interrupt, questioning where these bodies would come from, whether they are alive, and if we have to alter their state of being. He answers quickly without blinking an eye. I try not to let him know I can feel the coldness or separation in his non-reaction to my discomfort. I suppose my body language tells some of the story. If he knows me even a little, he knows I won't take a life, or would I? Have I? Yes, maybe in self-defense, unintentionally while backed against a wall. I don't think many people wouldn't want to live when faced with a life-or-death situation. I decide to hold my other question until the end.

He explains the bodies are already on ice, which sends a chill down my spine. The bodies were stolen from a nearby medical lab which, by the way, never reported them missing. They were involved in some unauthorized experiments, but someone gave them the thumbs up to the madness. The bottom line would be that it is wrong, immoral—unethical is the word I'm looking for. In short, I don't think they want to explain missing bodies.

I think he put some real thought into this because he goes on. I'm listening and in deep thought, asking myself: How far would I go to steal nineteen billion dollars from organized secret society-type families who specialize in capital gains and its redistribution? He goes on to say the job payout for the MAN would be around a hundred billion. The red tape that comes in the aftermath would net The Powers That Be in the hundreds of billions. If war should break out over all of this, they clock a cool billion a week in above-board, legitimate government contracts.

As we discuss war, I ask him if he thinks the government is behind all this, or if it's just some bad apples. I also wonder if those bad apples are being funded by the government—cartels, rogue leaders, tyrants, or totalitarianism hidden behind fake democratic voting machines.

He takes longer than I expect to answer what I think is a simple yes or no question. During that time, my mind races into overdrive, pondering the fallout of a venture of this magnitude. Some companies in the red will be pulled back from bankruptcy with under-bid, over-budget cost practices due to unforeseen circumstances, of course. Most of the public won't see the increased spending until it's nearly finished. They're afraid to say, "No, let's not spend more good money after bad money because of the 'it's too late to turn back now' attitude." The news networks will only report what the owners of the networks allow them to.

The headlines will read something like, "The Projected Budget for War has been Mismanaged and Understated." As you read further into the rhetoric, they hope you don't see that the war will cost the taxpayers a trillion dollars instead of a few hundred billion. Since the war isn't being run from your front door directly, you Joe, and Jane, the people say nothing out loud. Why? Because you are one of the ones benefiting from said government contracts, or if overheard talking against the new deal, you will be seen as against us and detained as a combatant versus a citizen exercising your freedom of speech. All it takes is one phone call misunderstood or they know exactly what you're saying but The Powers That Be want you to stop talking. Before you know it, THEY are at your front door and putting you away in some foreign country, sleeping and eating in a box smaller than you until they decide you've had enough of speaking out. You think about it, but you are afraid to escape because you realize you are no longer in America. This is detained, the term of time is indefinite and who wants to go through that?

Okay so, they decide you are an American and give you your phone call. You call your lawyer and they put her in jail for helping you. This will send the unspoken message to all lawyers to pick a side; if you're not with us, you are against us. The system has cloned the politicians as puppets, with the wealthiest one percent pulling the strings on both sides of the war, and the red tape that goes along with that will become its own oversight committee. Now it's out of sight and soon out of the public's mind. The world would have been close to its end by the time we really got around to asking the unanswered questions again.

Cleo breaks my train of thought. "I don't care who's behind it at all. They're stealing it and we're stealing it back. I wish I could take more but after a few billion in my pocket to spread around, wanting more would just be greedy, and make us one of them. We just want to be small brush strokes in the background of the big picture. The applied color we're going to make won't even be noticed by the undiscerning eye. If all goes as planned, they will create a masterpiece. Let's say that differently, only God can create. They will make a masterpiece while trying to be a master race. No, not a master race like people of color, more like a cadre of people who've managed to accumulate massive assets. The haves and the have-nots are, at best, the wall this work of art will be displayed on."

We walk into the towers and it's getting late. Most of the stores are closed, and I've never been here before, so I am not getting the full impact from a building like this. In fact, I've never been inside the Sears Tower, and I've spent a lot of years in Chicago. I'm sure a lot of people are in the same shoes, not visiting the main tourist sights of the towns they've lived in for most of the year.

I wonder how far this building goes into the ground. It has subway train tracks running right through it. This tour is done. I suppose Cleo has all the information he needs. The Tower is still standing, and we are still breathing in the same time zone and space we walked into the building with. My dream doesn't seem to be telling me about the future at this point. As we get back to the car, the streets seem quiet, and the same for the ride back to the club. I guess the thought of having a billion dollars at your disposal is turning out to be a tall task.

Deep thought is the price to pay for having truckloads of money to spend. Cleo takes a minute to run down a few more details and ends by saying the original plan should easily overshadow what we're doing. They have already considered a margin of error, so we would be giving them one. By my count, I come up with a few banks, a couple of gold exchanges, and the same for diamond shops, not counting what may be in a safe deposit box. I make a mental note during our walkthrough.

Now at the club, I don't recognize any of the spoken word artists. I like listening; the words make me consider what I could say on a subject. Cleo asks if I want to play pool or chess. I ask if we can play chess with the new rules. Hey says no, so we shoot pool.

The announcer introduces the next artist. A little time goes by, and the MC figures the artist is a no-show. The MC says, "The Double Dutch will take this moment to give to anyone who has anything to say about whatever you want. You can say it now. Do I have any takers?"

"Me," I say.

"We have a taker or a giver; it depends on how we look at it, so give Me some love as he extends his emotion, exposes his expression, fresh off the pressures of his experience. Send Me to the stage."

It's as if I am an old pro at this. I step onto the stage and outside of myself, watching me go at it.

Letter to my sons and my daughters and any child and their friends I've yet to recognize.

Time goes by fast and slow, all at the same time.

It stops and resets itself on a continuous loop, and it reveals all things, eventually.

Yes, time will tell and in an instant the time has passed.

If not for wisdom, caution, to wait, look, listen, then go,
You can miss your time to shine.

You can't go back in time.

Learn the signs and be prepared this time, the next time is near.

You can start now and again, but be mindful to use time well,
One doesn't get much to spend, and it can cost you your fortune in the end.

Get up and do something, go somewhere or you may be sent,
Doing the right thing makes a difference in time wasted or time well spent.

We will all have bad times; good times too and by the grace of God, bad will be few.

Most of the time life is just passing through.

By the time you work for food, rent or mortgage, phone, clothes, toilet paper,

or plastic, water, a cold one, or a shot. Give God a 10th and then some,

Pay yourself some or the same, most of the time not in that order,

So, at the right time you can have some fun.

Instead of spending time thinking about what you should have taken care of by now.

And now it's time to go and do something else and it's no time for that right now.

I was given some time to say this, out of my time thinking about it.

Now I just have to find some time to write it down. I sit here passing time,

As I pass gas to a higher place, it stinks. It sinks

I give the time of my day to you, for what it's worth. I was asked to fill in the time,

My science on time I felt I could pass on, and it only took a moment to listen,

I hope you find it was a good use of your time.

Me leaves the stage to fingers popping.

CHAPTER 11

What Goes Around Comes Around

I could have this confession end here, with many unanswered questions, having you imagine the outcome. What would you do, or would have done in either case, filling in the blanks, even the redistribution of a few billion dollars? Unfinished business would be a good working title. No? Okay, I don't want to do that. What would Jesus do? I don't think Jesus would have Himself in this situation. Maybe what would King David do? Please allow Me to handle my business.

I mean, what's really good for Me? Faced with the process, it becomes its own dilemma. Let me take care not to become lost in the procedure of picking on the process.

Where am I? Where did I get this watch which counts backwards? What's important to Me but may not be important enough to carry what I'm saying forward or even be important to you. That sword will cut both ways in all situations.

What happened to Cleo's lady friend? Well, I can just tell you, she didn't make it. There is a memorial set up in front of the Double Dutch. This would be the place where the people who knew her best would want to be.

Okay, where did I get the watch? Well, after some questions, I found a shop. My watch has both the time going forward and counting down. The forward count is on a 2400-hour readout. For example: 1:00 p.m. equals 1300 hours, and 2:00 p.m. equals 1400 hours. The countdown reads in years, months, days, and hours. The digital reads as you press buttons. It has a long hand and a short hand for show. I really don't remember when I came upon this watch.

At first, I thought it was 2002, which would have been when I started hearing of the second or third coming of the world ending. In case you haven't heard, the world has been ending for some time now. Harold Camping, a talk radio host put this latest end date in place with a Biblical theme.

A watch that counts forward and backward makes me feel the universe is caving in on itself, like back from the future and away from the past at once. May 21, 2011, at 11:00 am Eastern Standard Daylight Savings Time and all that. The present time to the end is 947,876 minutes to the end, or 7 months. 12 days, 11 hours, or just 224 days, or 5376 hrs., or just 322,560 minutes, or 19,353,000 seconds, as of 10/10/10.

I remember another moment when Jim Jones and his group of followers drank Kool-Aid laced with poison. That incident taught me the importance of critically examining things before accepting them without question, as Jim Jones and his group of followers misled people into believing a false truth. There were men, women, and children who drank, and were all found dead on the day after the end of the world had not come.

You get these kinds of results if you're lost, and don't understand what you think you know. Then you make decisions without counsel from the Word of God with wisdom and understanding.

It's unfortunate when the Bible is used to justify such a deadly end. All Christians should be clear on the things of God as it pertains to life and His return. I said all that to bring up more of this. Harold Camping and others who believe as he does, call into his radio show asking questions about the Bible, the end of the world, and Jesus' return are popular subjects.

The King James Version, as the living Word of God, answers these questions by Harold Camping and others who believe as he does. Most people call in and ask him to read where the Word of God says, *But of that day and hour no man knows, no, not the angels in Heaven, but the Father only.* Mr. Camping would say, "He told Noah and because God is the same today, yesterday, and forever, He will tell us."

Mr. Camping has booklets that show how he came up with findings through the Bible. He bases his beliefs on the Bible, asserting that God has not used churches since 1988 because of the devil's influence, and highlighting the appointment of individuals with alternative lifestyles to the Word of God as pastors in some American pulpits. The Word of God tells us that wisdom *is the principal thing; therefore, get wisdom, and in all you're getting, get understanding.*

The moral fiber of the church is coming apart. I've heard it said that we've become focused on the way we worship versus becoming more focused on the reason we worship and who we worship. Jesus the Christ is worthy of our praise. The fear of God is the beginning of wisdom. In all your getting, get understanding. Our brain is not little or tiny, it's wonderfully made along with our body. The word of God says, ask God what you will. He will not leave you ignorant. Our ways are not His ways, our thoughts are not His thoughts, and it does not mean the children of God cannot understand the word of God.

Misunderstanding is the dilemma of the children of wrath. For instance, I may have thoughts of a gold brush and comb, or toilet seat, but only in the Bible are the streets made of gold, and now my mind can see it because my mind is not too small that I cannot comprehend. Why would God ask us to ask Him when we have questions if we can't understand the answers He gives us? The Bible says we are the sons of is just too much going on.

They turn and I think they hear me, but they are responding to someone else's cry. "I'm up here!"

I will give it another try. It's hot. The firefighters are leading people somewhere, maybe they know a way out. Some people are walking, some being carried.

The blast has collapsed the wall in many places and broken glass, twisted beams, and bars amongst everything else is everywhere. There is store merchandise all over the floor mixed in with concrete-marble-like tiles. Diamonds, gold chains, and bracelets, the watch I had right there, a metal rod through it and not my wrist. There is one like mine in a white gold or platinum design, tossed into the rubble as well.

Destruction is all I can see for as far as the concrete dust in the air will allow me to see. The temperature is too hot for most and they also collapse like the walls have fallen around them. Some are finding their strength gone, and all that remains is the will to live. It's incredible to see that even in the face of death, one can find a trinket, one of which they wouldn't have been able to afford otherwise and make their own.

I'm yelling, "Run for your life!" I think they hear me, maybe. One lady stands straight up from her picking, hopefully coming to her senses, and runs. Overcome by heat and greed, she tries to grab more items and loses a shoe. She can't find it in the mix of other shoes, some still attached to feet and some legs, pieces of everything everywhere. She moves on with one shoe over the mixture of glass, metal rods, and concrete, all twisted and broken.

She falls behind but sees the exit sign where everyone had gone, all hoping it was their way out. She makes it to the door, but the handles are too hot to touch. The firefighters are moving on with the others and are out of her sight. All she can do is move on, take a chance, and stay at the door, hoping they return. Her foot is bleeding more, and she loses track of the items she picked up.

I see firefighters and police officers trying to manage bodies on a stretcher. I'll wait until they're closer to me, then yell, "Help! I'm up here, help!" They stop but don't look up. They pass me by, so before they are out of reach, I give it another shout. They stop and look all around but not up.

The firefighters carrying the last stretcher stop to adjust their grip on the handles. When the lead man thinks he hears the okay to move on, he does just that. After a few steps, he notices the task has become harder to handle. He looks back and sees his partner has stopped to put something in his pocket. At that moment, the lead firefighter witnesses the ceiling collapsing on his partner.

He sees his partner is still alive and goes back to help, but there's too much concrete and steel to move without help. In this situation, their training involves the use of spray paint to mark the location of a fallen comrade. They mark the location of a fallen comrade by placing an "X" on the nearest standing wall or the ground.

He runs back to the wounded man on the stretcher, who tells him he gave an engraved watch to the partner for his family in case he doesn't survive. The lead firefighter tries to process if his partner is really under a pile of rubble because of a watch. It takes everything in him to keep a blank face while he picks up the stretcher and pulls it behind him alone. No good deed goes unpunished.

I'm still trying to focus through the ash. I notice similar marks guiding the next wave of rescue personnel to other fallen rescuers last seen alive. An X marks the spot. An X on the ground or a tree has historically been used to mark the place where a Christian died for the cause of Christ.

Melted metal from steel beams is flowing from the upper floors like volcano lava, burning everything in its path, and I am feeling the heat. I feel someone pulling my leg up from where I am, and now I'm in a cool place. I hear a voice, but I can't figure out who is talking. There's a ringing in my ear, and it's getting louder and louder.

"Sorry, ladies and gentlemen, we are experiencing some technical difficulties," the announcer says.

O.M. walks into a booth in the back in the dark, and I seem to be awake now from dreaming. I'm at the end of my rope from not sleeping as I should. Even when I fall asleep, it feels like I'm awake somewhere else. My brain stays active, making up stuff on its own.

I catch up with Cleo across the club and let him know I'm out of there, telling him I'll see him later. Since I fell asleep in the club, I figure it's best to leave. I hope the nap I had there is enough to get me to Cleo's place to crash.

As I hit the road, the bright lights come back on, and once again, I have no idea where they are coming from. The sounds of people talking make me turn off the CD player and ensure all the windows are up. I'm alone now with my thoughts, good or bad. I have yet to figure it out.

I wonder if the police have finished the investigation. Am I still a prime suspect? I'm not front-page news now, so it's hard to see what the press knows. I guess I should check in and ask, but she was cheating, so how much do I really care? I'm good if they don't pin it on me.

I know I'm a big guy, but do they think I have the strength to take the head off a man with no weapon and no blood on me anywhere or something? I know I lived there, and that alone gives me the opportunity, and what I saw gives me motive.

The only question remaining is, am I capable?

They have no witnesses, no weapon, and no head—not that it matters, because they do have the bodies. Think about it, there's a bodiless head out there waiting to be found. Perhaps someone already found it, but some sicko is just kicking it around, not realizing it's real. No, that can't happen because of the smell of rotting flesh. The average person would notice something is wrong. It would surely look bad by now.

However, someone slightly below average might be attracted to this foul-smelling, awful-looking piece of something with eyes, believing they can save it and use it later to authenticate their haunted house on Halloween night. No, okay, maybe not.I call Cleo and let him know I need a change of scenery. I'm thinking of a hotel or Joy's place to spend some time with River. I'll call her and see if I can sleep in a guest room for a long nap.

"Hello, Joy, it's me. I need a favor."

"Sure anything."

"I'm hoping you can put me up in the guest room for a minute. Cleo's pull-down spare bed is cool, but a real bed would be better. What do you say?"

"Of course, you're welcome to it. I have a key over the door in case we're not in when you arrive. Let yourself in."

"Thanks."

I'm glad she said yes, and with a change in direction, I arrive at her place. I ring the doorbell even though I don't see her car. Right, no one's home. I open the door and walk in; I guess she forgot to lock it.

I try to lock the door behind me, but there's no key for the deadbolt. Then I remember the key is outside over the door. Okay, I'm in, and the house is secure because, you know, there's a killer out there.

I kick off my shoes and realize she didn't say which room was the guest room. Okay, there's a yellow room with River's stuff in it, an eggshell near white with Joy's stuff, and another room, light blue with a desk and a bed for me.

She left a bright light on in the middle of the high ceiling, which seems higher than the other ceilings in the house. I turn off the light and take off my socks, shirt, and pants, and I can't believe how good I know this is going to feel.

Oh, and yes, a bed, a real bed made up just like Mom used to make. I toss a little, warm up the sheets, and cover my head with one eye looking at the digital clock on the wall.

I see zero years, zero months, three days, ten seconds, nine, eight, seven, six, five, four, three, two, one. The last time I saw one of those doomsday clocks, it had a lot more time than that. Maybe I can set it to count down to anything, like the cooking timers on the stove.

I hear voices. Maybe Joy and River are back.

"How long do you think he'll be sleeping?" River asks.

"I don't know. When we spoke last, he said he needed rest," Joy answers. "I wish we could talk to him."

"Me, too, but you go and finish your fruit cocktail and maybe we can talk to him later." "The doctor said it could be a day or twenty-one days before he comes back," she mumbles under her breath.

"What did you say?"

She clears her throat. "Daddy may be sleeping for a long time or a little while. It's hard to tell."

Am I hearing them right? They're talking like I've been laying here for days. I just laid down. It sounds like I'm in a coma or something. I wonder how long I've been like this. I asked her to pull the plug if I was going to be a vegetable after waking up and couldn't actually wake up.

River turns and walks away. I'm apparently still inside myself.

I hear my daughter talking. "Do you think if I leave the light on, he'll wake up? It could happen."

As she walks out of the room, she flips on the light. Light pours into the bedroom window at Joy's house. It's the same kind of light Cleo and I saw earlier. I don't know if I'm trying to wake up or about to walk into my next life.

How am I seeing the light? I'm at a crossroads, a fork in the road. Can I run away from the light and stay in my present state of mind?

On one hand, I could be on trial for murder, though they have a weak case. I used to have a cheating wife, but now I don't, which is why I'm on trial.

I may be rich beyond my dreams if I can stay away from the people Cleo and I are stealing from. We've justified our actions by stealing from those planning to redistribute the world's wealth by collapsing the World Trade Center.

I'll be rich but constantly running, looking over my shoulder for the rest of my life, which wouldn't be restful at all. And if they piece it all together, it points to us.

CHAPTER 12

Half a Dozen in the Other

River seems to be in both worlds; the downside is they're coming after her and Joy. So much for a new life with her. Who brought River to the doctor, if I'm actually in a hospital and not just dreaming about being in a coma or all of this? Doors are literally opening up for me here. I have a question. If I'm caught by the authorities for crimes of passion or stealing and locked away in a jail cell, will I not be able to run towards the light if it always appears on the other side of the jail cell bars? At this point, I'm locked away inside my mind, waiting for someone to pull the plug. What if the rapture happens, and I leave this body, but the doctors don't know I've been raptured away, so I become some weird experiment for the people left behind? No, okay.

Joy comes in. "Wake up. You seem like you were having some kind of nightmare."

She shakes me a little to wake me. Now we are eye to eye as I focus. She kisses my lips, and again I think I'm dreaming. The bright light is gone now. Maybe I'm in some kind of coma state, and it's the nurse who kisses me to wake me. I guess she believes in fairy tales. After being unsuccessful, she leaves and turns out the light.

I leave it up to me to say, "Joy, I don't know what I was thinking or even if I should say anything. My mind and my heart are broken, and the cracks are still open. I wouldn't want you to fall through the pieces before I had some time to heal."

Joy looks at me in silence, trying to process what she just said or did. I'm not sure if it was Joy who kissed me or the nurse; I'm falling deeper and deeper into the rabbit hole.

Let me try to explain some of the cracks in my mind now that you see what's on my heart. If I'm right, in three days, according to the clock on the wall, the world is going to begin to end as we know it, not in the sense of the rapture or maybe so. I may go to jail for the murder of my wife, or I'll be involved in the biggest, greatest event ever to happen on American soil. On that great and terrible day, every American, and eventually the world will be affected. I'll become wealthy in the process, billionaire status. I mean, if you're going to steal, your actions should at least change your life, because if you get caught, your life will go through some changes.

The clear and present danger will affect the way we do everything in America forever. The fallout causes the economy to spin out of control. People will compare it to the Great Depression of the 1920s. As we recover, the government will allocate billions of dollars to cover it up. Meanwhile, thieves will make off with hundreds of billions in cash, gold, diamonds, bonds, and the like. A war is now justified. Accusers accuse a country of possessing weapons that will be used in another attack on American soil. Never mind that the ruler in question had nothing to do with the last attack. This lie will later be uncovered, but not until it has accomplished what it was sent out to do; and that is to confuse the people. The truth, for most, is even harder to believe. This was payback on a personal level. They brought a foreign country under their reign and killed its dictator.

Joy chimes in. "I know that train of thought will be reported widely in the media."

"Yes, but you don't know this execution was carried out because he didn't like his cut of the redistribution of wealth considering the part he had to play. For The Powers That Be, this was not good. To keep the unbelievable from coming to the light, even if it was coming from a source with no credibility, they did the unthinkable by killing the family of said dictator.

"Gangsta only begins to describe the magnitude of the many players involved. They wanted the world to belong to them and they don't want to share. The backlash would make way sooner rather than later to happen. We believe yes, but never in my lifetime. The reality of America's first Black President was just the thing, but for who? Who, I ask, made this so? My one vote amongst many or The Powers That Be? I know what most would hope but consider this; it will play perfectly in the plan of the well-to-do. It puts the blame of further losses to all the classes, in jobs and foreclosed homes onto the next person to hold that office no matter what color or gender they are.

"As a result of the negative light the media shines on African Americans, the world stage sees the US in a different, not so bright light. In the event of only one term in office or two, when the ink dries it says, America's worst moment in time was while a black President was in office, and any recovery will be given to the next person in office, as was the blame for the passing on of a failed policy from the last President. Let's say the next President is Black."

Joy is upset now. "So my vote meant nothing?"

"If it makes you feel better to think so, then think so. I vote and let it be said I did my part in case it does matter." Joy sighs heavily and sits in dismay while listening intensely.

"There were some changes made because of a Black president in office. To get the money back into the hands of the people, a few laws were passed. Black Americans received compensation for their role in building the foundation of our great nation. Black Americans who qualified for their college of choice had their bills paid as long as they lived on campus. Another bill passed was the Reflection. It intended to have America's Commander-in-Chief look more like the people who voted him or her into office. Considering the law, to run for the president's office, one must have a race other than white in their family tree. In other words, the one drop of black or brown blood rule was required to run.

"This law did not sit well with the all-white voters and others that take their whiteness to the extreme. Oddly enough, this proved not to be an issue in the next elections. Every candidate seeking the office met the criteria of having a person of color in their family tree. Another law was passed with the intent of letting as many people as possible work. The military was given a pay increase. This meant that the members that were married could only have one breadwinner in the home and could not hold a second job. Married with no children had to choose which one would attend school to prepare for life being discharged from the military. Unmarried members could not hold a second job if they were full-time members of the armed forces and could go to school. The minimum wage was raised to meet the cost of living on a state-by-state basis. A second breadwinner in a home was taxed at a different rate if found out."

Joy questions, "What about young men and women working but still living at home?"

"If the income cannot sustain that person outside the home, they are taxed at a decreased rate, looking at them as a second income for the home they're living in. The assumption would be that a person would not be living at home rent free. I restated that this change would mostly be for service members. Finally, all weapons made on a given date, to be announced, cannot have an automatic fire selection on any gun or rifle. All load and reload clips can only hold 11 bullets maximum, and one in the chamber."

Joy is not feeling my "If I Were King" speech. "Good luck with that."

"The military was the best place to start such a thing because it is easy to regulate. The hope would be that the rest of the US would soon enough get on board. All of us must start somewhere sacrificing something so more of us can have a little. As the term living wage takes the place of the term minimum wage, hope in the future won't be as hard to find. Face it, because you are a part of the United States of America's Armed Forces, you shouldn't need a second job to provide for your family."

Joy pauses. "But you paint such a dark yet somewhat hopeful picture right now. You would think in present times people could go past the skin and not let the way I feel about another race or think on a particular matter stop us from being productive as a nation. As it is, that moment in time is not now. Not everyone is willing to share."

"As a result of all the changes, the following happened:

First, some southern states broke away from the union. The new way of life coming out of the White House is not sitting well. New Orleans, Texas, and Mississippi declared their independence, oil being the source which maintains their economy.

"Freshwater had become the thing to have and sell or protect if you had it on the land you owned. Others were considering the options of separating from the union.

"California still had some untapped gold reserves, along with South America, that had newly discovered gold caves the size of ten football fields. They estimate a twenty-four-hour operation produces three thousand gold bars every day for ten years into the future.

"If we are still here and have not destroyed ourselves, the present road system in that county can pave the roads with gold, which would be a waste of resources and a far cry from streets being made of gold.

"The streets are made of gold inside the cave and the place is fondly called little heaven. When these states and others declare independence, the world stage will look a little different. I know it's a lot to take in, but I'm thinking about it, and that's all I can say about that."

Joy gets up and paces the floor.

"As for Cleo and Open Mic, and what happened to me, it is just another part of my version of God's goodness, mercy, favor, and His judgment.

What would be strong enough to pull the head off the human body since no weapon was found?

These characters being so much a part of me have taken on the physical form and are always encamped around me. The downside of this would be it's just me and faced with a dilemma, my defense mechanisms became a form outside of me. The transformation is seamless and without effort or conscious thought, I don't even notice even though I can see them in operation. Other situations I've noticed but not mentioned, I can't explain, only God knows. Earth, blood, wind, tears, sweat, and fire.

"Now that I realize all of this, I must give you some bad news about you. You, Joy, are not real right now. You are a real friend from my younger years. The only reason I suppose you're here is because I remember you and what we had. You are a great moment in my life of wishful thinking, and you have left an impression. Are you getting all of this?"

Joy looks into my eyes with wide eye attentiveness. "Well, if I have it right, what can I say? You must tell me what to tell you.

Joy stops talking for a minute, and then says, "Run toward the light. River and I will be okay. Next time you see the light, run to it. You may wake up or find out the light is everything everyone thinks it is, heaven's doorway. In which case, I'll see you when I get there. As it stands now, the question remains. Where is that head?"

CHAPTER 13

I think for a minute before answering the questions. Do I know where the head is? Could a part of me be having an out-of-body experience or going temporarily insane? This would explain some things and be a good, tried-and-true defense in situations like this—insanity. What disturbs me is, if it's true, I don't remember. Am I capable of this kind of crime in the future? What I remember is turning on the camera, but I won't say anything about that. Afterward, I back out of the room, down the stairs, and out the door to sit on my front steps.

Cleo pulls up to talk about his girl until I tell him what's going on with me and why I'm sitting on the steps. After talking, he tells me we're leaving and that I should follow him. I ask him to go inside to get my shoes and keys because I don't think I can handle going back inside. All I need is right there as you come through the door.

I don't know how long it takes him to do this. It seems like a few seconds, even if it's twenty minutes. That moment remains etched in my mind. I remember putting on my shoes, and we are out of there. I follow him back to the club, not knowing why. Then he tells me to call home and say I'm at the club. I remember leaving a message. As for the camera, either could have secretly turned it on to record the act without the other knowing. The judgment of God is what I find the next day, and the police have my statement and the camera. I guess we'll see soon enough if the camera caught what happened in that room.

"To answer your question, Joy, yes, it's all in my head, so I'll be alright. I just have to believe in my mind that I will win in the end."

The only truth I can say is the truth I know. Believing it is the trick. Easy enough to do, which is why lie detectors are no longer used in court as evidence. A deeper mode in the subconscious has to be influenced; that I may never forget what I said to the police. Forgetting will allow doubt to take root. This way, the court can never consider the whole truth of the matter again. The truth being I was there, but I didn't do the crime. I believe in my heart and mind that I'm not capable of such an act.

Riddle me this? We often hear the phrase, speak your mind; so, who's in control, the heart or mind when the heart has a voice? Let's say I lost my mind, and then whose mind was I thinking with? YOU'VE JUST ENTERED THE TWILIGHT ZONE. Come out of there!

Of course, if I say I was there, even if they never find a murder weapon, I think a jury would find me guilty. Let's say some kind of way I did the crime as long as I never remember a jury trial. You can never believe a lie you've told yourself because your subconscious will always replay the truth, therefore in my dreams or wide awake, someone will always ask me about what happened that night. They, a detective in my mind, can't shake the feeling that they've missed something that will bring out the truth. You see, the actors in your mind every day in real life. The real me knows he has withheld information, and he's trying to keep that information from his subconscious. Okay, look at it this way; I'm trying to convince myself that the lie I'm telling is true. What is done in the dark will come to the light.

At this point, I'm the judge, jury, court reporter, prosecution, and the accused. I sit all over the courtroom, seeing remembered faces as the audience for the hearing, and the grasshopper that keeps flying in and out of the courtroom window. A house divided can never stand. That which I know is wrong to do, I do. The heart is deceitful above all things and desperately wicked. Who can know what I'm thinking? You can only know how you hope to react in any situation. The parts of my brain—eighty-five to ninety percent we believe we can't use—may have consequences. Could I still find myself declared guilty and thrown in jail, unable to run toward the light if I see it?

Joy still doesn't have much to say. She smiles, then stands up, saying, "Get some rest."

I lay down and close my eyes. I can't say the same for the activity in my brain, it's wide awake. *We're all on a particular path.*

You don't have to know what lies ahead to sow with your gift.

We're born before the beginning with the one that knows the ending.

So, I look out to see, trying to make it better for you and me, as we reap.

I know I sound funny at times because I talk about money and having it in abundance.

We need it to operate on this plane.

Not to love it, but to use it, share it, plant it in good ground and God will allow you to make more of it.

With power from heaven, I get spiritual, showing you the real me.

I'm watching my father and mother use the mixture, making the heart of an Obama, or Jordan.

So, I've discovered that I'm not like Mike.

I'm the original me and I can see higher than he can fly.

Being voted in to be president would be a good thing, but wouldn't that be a step down from being born kings and priests?

The truth of God has made me free.

The Comforter gives power for praise and prayer. He pushes potential for the great purpose of teaching the principles of Jesus with passion and persistence.

Determined, motivated, and inspired to make my dedication better.

To reach the chosen and help us live by what we speak on and believe in.

I pledge not to let myself down.

Reading the Word of I AM, we learn about a life we can have at the top and not the bottom, in front and not behind.

It's okay to put your hand in mine, for the Jesus in me will never let you go.

As one looks back on my life, I hope they'll say, 'He prayed to have the blind and deaf, see and hear of The Jesus.

When I open my mouth, mostly the things of God will come out.

Yes, knowing me won't get you to heaven, but accepting Jesus the Christ in me, you will never die the second death. AMEN.

Now at the trial, they present all the standard pieces of evidence but toss them because I live there. My lawyer points out that not presenting the evidence would have raised an eyebrow. They question the prints from my fingers on the digital camera the most. At the moment in question, only four people have access to it: my wife, the adulterer, the intruder, and me. Each of us has an interest in recording the scene. Why capture the moment? For me, it serves as proof.

For the intruder, a warning. The adulterer would keep it as a trophy, and my wife would use it to relive her torrid affair. I stick to my story that I didn't push the record button. I state again, it's my house and my camera, so, of course, my prints are on it. Now it's time to see the tape made from the camera that they put into evidence.

The prosecution points out, "I'm going to remind you that the footage you are about to see is graphic and contains nudity. The fingerprints on the camera that captured these images are without question the prints of the accused. It is his camera, found in his house, and at the time of crimes committed."

My lawyer objects. "This is not proof he was there at the time."

The footage starts with two people doing what married couples do when they've become one, often resulting in offspring. Then a large figure enters the frame. The angle only shows from the knees up to the shoulders and some neck. The intruder goes unnoticed by the couple at first, but then she turns around, maybe to look into the camera or because of that feeling we all get when someone is watching. The paranoid feeling is overwhelming, especially when doing something you shouldn't. She turns and screams, loud and chilling, causing a woman in the jury box to scream and faint suddenly. This disrupts the courtroom, and the judge calls for order. The tape stops, and we adjourn for a short recess.

We return and stand as the judge enters, then sit. The tape replays, and we hope we're prepared for what we'll see. We aren't. It's the same as before: the people, the intruder, the scream, but then silence as if someone hit the mute button. There are no indicators showing the mute function, causing more disruption. People talk among themselves, asking what happened. Is this a malfunction in the court equipment or the camera, or just part of it all?

The judge brought the room to order with the banging of his gavel, and the tape continued. Now the other person is involved, and you can see the shock on his face. His eyes widened, lips were moving, and a terrified look on her face remained and open mouths as if to scream, but no sound comes from them as they take in the figure's massiveness at the end of the bed. Before he can react to the situation, he's pulled off the bed and thrown to the floor. He gets to his feet, and it looks as if he's going to fight, but after some thought, he looks around to pick up something to fight with. He grabs an elephant-shaped paperweight and begins moving side to side. With a burst of energy he lunges at the intruder, but to no avail. It merely seemed like he was running into the intruder's arms for a dance of the tango. The adulterer tried to use the weapon, but the free arm is now pinned to his side. At first, it looked like the tango, and we were right to think of them dancing. The intruder had the adulterer under such submission that only his head could move in his defense.

He used it to head butt the intruder, and it had no effect. It looked like kisses.

In the darkness captured by the camera, we see the intruder. He spins around gracefully with an unwilling partner in what becomes the adulterer's last dance. The wife tries to run but gets hit hard in the face by the dancers' outstretched arms and is tossed back onto the bed in a daze. The intruder continues to dance with the seemingly lifeless body as the wife gathers herself. She gets onto her knees on the bed and watches as the intruder, still holding the adulterer's wrist, lets it go. He reaches over with the same hand, placing it at the adulterer's neck on the right side with his thumb pointing down. In the blink of an eye, the adulterer's head suffers a gruesome decapitation. The entire courtroom is in shock; no one moves to shut off the tape. Blood pumps from the lifeless body as the intruder spins another turn, holding the body in one arm and the head in his right hand.

Some people lose their lunch and others faint all over the courtroom. The wife is still on her knees and can't believe her eyes. Like us in the courtroom, she cannot move. In the intruder's completion, the head hurls toward the wife with force, hitting the wife in her upper torso just below her neck. Although there is no sound, one could imagine the ribs or collarbone cracking and then breaking. I do. Considering decapitation with no weapon, the head hurled at top speed, akin to something unnatural. The impact of the head knocks her into the wall, causing her to fall off the bed and onto the floor between the bed and the wall nearest the corner of the room, with one foot still in the frame with a big toe pressed against the wall.

There is no more movement, and the footage doesn't show the head's final resting place after bouncing off the wife. It shows the head moving out to the left of the camera shot. We can't see how the intruder gets away, or when authorities retrieved the head. The camera plays a few more minutes until the low battery warning begins to flash and soon turns itself off.

What we have just seen aligns with what the press released. According to the paper, they found two murdered bodies, one decapitated, and they couldn't find either the murder weapon or the head at the scene. After stopping the tape, the lawyers begin their opening statements.

In America, the state has the uphill burden of proof. They lead off with a reading of an interview with my daughter about what she remembers about what happened; she was not present in court. I guess they did this to show the danger she was in, but not harmed because she's my daughter. If it wasn't for me, maybe she would have been a third victim. The short version is when she woke up and went to our bedroom, the door was locked. She knocked, and there was no answer. We taught her that in case of emergency, go to the list on the refrigerator and start calling the numbers listed from the top down until you reach someone. I'm first on the list, then the wife, and 911, then close neighbors and nearby relatives, and so on. She called my cell. She gave me the details, and I told her not to worry, sit and have milk and cereal in front of the TV, and if I'm not there in one hour, call the number 4 person on the list, the next-door neighbor, a retired couple who agreed to be on our list. There was no need to call them, as I was there in forty-eight minutes.

Now I'm on the stand and under oath—or am I? I refuse to put my hand on the Bible to be sworn in. To whom am I obligated to tell the truth? Only to God the Father in heaven. It's a commandment from on high. A Christian knows to tell the truth without swearing or making vows, especially with a hand on the Bible. That's not appropriate for a believer. When considering everything that pertains to me, I wonder why the Bible is the standard in the world's courtroom. Nonbelievers have no obligation to the word of God, for they are of their father, the devil, being unsaved. Christians, however, are forgiven for the sin of lying because of what Jesus Christ did on the cross.

I affirm. The judge instructs the prosecution to proceed with questioning. He has only one question for now: "Have you broken any laws getting to your daughter?" I answer, "Yes." He has no further questions. That question establishes the fact that I will do or say whatever I need to, even if it goes against the law. My lawyer asks me to tell my story.

"Okay, I got a call from my daughter saying she couldn't wake up her mommy, nor could she open the bedroom door. That's when I left work. I gave her instructions on what to do until I got there. When I arrived, I found her sitting in front of the TV eating cereal and milk and cookies. The cookies were her idea. I said to stay there. I was going up to see what happened to mommy. She said, 'Okay,' and I went up. I opened the door to the room and saw the mess. A naked male body with his head laying on the floor. While still holding onto the doorknob, I looked around in the back of the door and saw the foot against the wall coming off the bed. I closed the door while walking backward. While I tried not to go into shock over what I saw and being mad over the same, then to thank God for letting whoever came in overnight didn't see my little girl sleeping, or he did see her and spared her life."

All the time, the real truth plays in my head while I fabricate the story I'm sticking to. I thought they were alive when I left, after pushing the button on the camera, of course. Was the intruder already there? I don't know what to think after seeing what the camera caught.

CHAPTER 14

Sticking to My Story

I continue with my facts and fiction mixture. "I stayed strong for my daughter. I dressed her in an outfit she picked and took her to school. I grabbed a few extra items because she wouldn't be back there anytime soon, if ever. I called the police as I walked back to the car after dropping River off at school. I told them to meet me at the house and gave them the address; I told them someone had been murdered. The 911 operator asked where I was and if I was alright. I told her I was okay, and I would meet the police at the location."

The prosecution asks how tall I am and if I can bench press my weight. These questions aim to establish that I could be the same height and possibly as strong as the intruder.

We continue after some objections from my lawyer. There's no real way to tell how tall the intruder is, so he

168

introduces a show-and-tell to the court—a kind of prop. It's a dummy with the same weight and height, made of material with the same resistance as skin, inner veins, muscle, and bone as the man whose head was pulled off his body, give or take a pound.

The prosecution objects, stating we don't know the weight and size of the man's head and neck because they were not found at the scene. My lawyer uses the average head size that would typically accompany a body of that size. The judge allows it.

My lawyer uses another prop: a bodybuilder. He and I weigh about the same, but he has much more muscle mass. His arms and legs are almost twice the size of mine. He is asked some questions for the record, including his name and what he does for a living, which is important because he is a professional kickboxer, making him suitable for the task. He appears menacing. He is to interact with the dummy to see if he can pull the head off the lifeless prop. This seems appropriate because, at the time of decapitation, the victim's body was limp, just hanging from the intruder's arms.

Everyone gets in place, and the reenactment begins. Moving like the intruder did, with his hands and arms positioned the same, the kickboxer cannot pull the head off the dummy. Objections arise, claiming the dummy is too big, and the kickboxer isn't trying his best because he's hired by the defense. My lawyer anticipates this and brings in a smaller dummy, considering the intruder might have had some unforeseen advantage. The kickboxer tries again but still fails.

The prosecution says he would like to try. The judge finds the request odd but allows it, perhaps thinking the prosecution lawyer would give it a go. Instead, the prosecution asks for a recess to resume the next day with someone on his payroll to try to pull the head from the dummy. The state doesn't believe our man is doing his best. The judge, along with everyone else in court, feels a little deceived because of the way the question is asked, not considering all that was answered. The judge pauses with a poker face, but his raised eyebrow shows he doesn't like what just happened. He still adjourns the court for the prosecution to find a large man to pull the head off the defense's prop. I take this opportunity to get some sleep—I'm exhausted.

It's the next day, and the trial resumes. My attorneys inform me that our investigators have found new evidence that doesn't go in my favor. They tell me my cell signal was tracked to and from the crime scene around the time of the murders. The only thing in my favor is testimony showing the time of death after I had returned to Club Double Dutch. We can only assume the other side has the same information and is waiting for the best time, if ever, to use it. This still only proves I was there, not that I did it. It gives me opportunity, but not capability or real motive. I could have come home, seen everything was well, and decided to go back out because I wasn't tired enough to go to bed and didn't want to wake up the whole house with the TV playing. I had just been paid—it was Friday.

We come to order, and the prosecution calls his next witness to the stand. To my surprise, and everyone else's, it's my wife, who was presumed dead but is very much alive. She's changed her hair to a bleached blonde color, but it's unmistakably her. I don't know how to react. I'm overwhelmed with a mix of emotions, trying to process this revelation. My lawyer objects, and it is explained that the fact of her being alive was kept secret for her safety. Due to the brutal nature of the crime and the killer not being caught, it was decided that it was easier to protect someone who was supposed to be dead. After all, who looks to harm a dead person?

I look around the court to see who is watching me try to maintain my best poker face while, in fact, still searching for emotion and hoping the poker face isn't counting against me. I mean, she was sleeping around, and even though I thought the way she died was cruel, I wouldn't have wished that on anyone. I don't think I'm different from anyone in wishing she was dead at that moment. Okay, I'm glad she's not dead, for River's sake. I wonder what she's going to say.

I wake up my lawyer being paged back to courtroom five. "Monarch, Esquire, Mercury Monarch, please report to courtroom five." Everyone is going back into the courtroom. Cleo and O.M. take their seats. I guess I must have fainted.

The state calls my wife to the stand. My lawyer objects again but is overruled. The judge wants to get to the bottom of all this.

The judge calls both lawyers to the bench, asking why a dead woman is in his courtroom. The state gives those reasons, and the judge allows it. My wife is sworn in, and it ends with, "I do," from her.

The state begins his line of questioning, going straight to the point. "Do you see the intruder in the courtroom today?" Her eyes scan the room back and forth twice. If she does see, she isn't saying; in fact, she isn't saying anything. She is asked again, but she remains silent, staring blankly at the back of the room, toward OM and Cleo. Since she says nothing, the judge orders everyone in the courtroom to leave except for the court reporter, one state lawyer, and one lawyer for me. I am also asked to leave. The judge then asks the witness if the intruder has left the room. Her response is the same; catatonic comes to mind. If God's evil angel is present, she has nothing to say about it. I guess she sees me and remembers what she did. She recalls who or what entered the room once sin was fully grown. She is thankful her life was spared, but the intruder could return at any time. It appeared without a sound and walked away into nothingness after the decapitating dance.

The thought apparently paralyzes her with fear. She is asked to step down, but she cannot move. A wheelchair is brought in, and she is carried to it and wheeled away while everyone stands along the halls of the courthouse, watching.

I am thinking to myself, *"Glad I didn't tell River her mother had left the land of the living. Now I can tell her that she can see her sometime in the future, as long as she doesn't mind the padded rooms, or sometimes see a person sitting with a straitjacket.*

We will wish her well, River and me. As for me, I can forgive; my spirit does that perfectly. My mind, on the other hand, is being renewed by the Word of God and still has moments of weakness. My mind reminds my body that it no longer wants anything to do with her. It tells me to protect myself from abuse. The God in me says stay, but my mind and body fear what it can do if attacked again, and that part of me does not wish the best for her. Of course, I could only understand if someone judged me the same. The Word gives us caution to that line of thinking. She was caught in the act of adultery, and until I change how I feel, I don't think I can change what I think. Maybe my thinking has to change first, and my feelings will follow in a little while. I asked myself, *How long is a little while, and will time heal this wound? Yes, we say that time heals, but I've yet to see.* Thank you, God, for forgiveness because a lot of me is so far from perfect.

Everyone is asked to come back into the courtroom. To my surprise, the lawyers have no more questions, despite the evidence from the cell phone records. Now, it is time for closing arguments. I guess the state couldn't find a strong man to pull the head off the lifelike dummy.

The state points out that I could have made that call from inside the house, suggesting I was too drunk to drive from the club once aware of what I had done. Records show the cell tower at the time of the call was near the club, referencing some phone records but not confident enough to put them into evidence. They also mention that people can display incredible strength during moments of stress caused by emergencies or blinding anger. They cite instances where people have been known to lift cars off their children or blackout and perform the unthinkable. "The heart is desperately wicked; who can know it?" he says, closing his arguments with, "I rest my case."

The defense points to the fact that, yes, people are known to do the unthinkable, but not the impossible. "The accused doesn't look as if he possesses the strength needed to perform the acts displayed in the video. The person in the video looks at least eight feet tall or more. The accused is six-feet-five inches in height at best.

The prosecution quotes from the Bible "Then consider if extra strength was given to the accused, as given onto Samson, God's Judge; would not the actions of the accused be ordained by The Father in Heaven? Who are we to second-guess God? The facts are no weapon, no witness, and no unexplained blood not being on the accused. If he did this crime of passion, he was temporarily insane, and you must acquit. He was not himself."

My lawyer, feeling pretty confident, asks if there are any phone records in question. I hold my breath. The state pauses and answers, "No." The judge gives the jury instructions and dismisses them to deliberate.

The jury has not come back by the end of the business day, so the judge dismisses everyone for dinner and resumes the following day.

Cleo, OM, and I discuss the details of what needs to come together in three days. If everything goes as planned, we will never look at life the same. Our part in the big picture involves getting lifeless, uniformed armored car drivers past the checkpoints. What's left of those bodies will be found in the armored car that doesn't get away, filled with cash, bonds, and bricks of gold and platinum. The intense heat will liquefy the metals, leaving only an estimated value. The authorities won't be able to determine if the bodies were dead before the fire or died in it. The Powers That Be will find us missing, and we will be labeled beyond recognition. The public will know only what *they* tell the networks to say. Questions will arise: "How did all these armored cars get here so fast? It's as if they were on standby."

Six cars are recovered by insurance agents, who receive commissions. Two cars are unaccounted for, and two are in our possession. The Powers That Be should have gotten those two armored cars from us, but we supposedly died in the ones found. The other armored car counts as a total loss in insurance claims, reimbursed to the owners of stores, banks, and the like. This armored car and two others are assumed to be part of the hot, lava-like flow at the bottom of the towers. That makes four cars in all, lost in the extreme heat.

The Powers That Be settle for two, while we have three out of the twelve cars used. Each car holds an estimated ten billion. The math says thirty billion to split between the three of us. As for The Powers That Be, they lose nothing. Looking at the big picture, The Powers That Be are the beneficiaries of the insurance policies.

Now that the pieces are in place, all we do is wait. I take a moment to sit because I'm having a hard time keeping my eyes open.

CHAPTER 15

The Beginning of the End

The jury is back, and they can't decide beyond a reasonable doubt. You guessed it—I'm innocent. They don't have enough evidence to convict me, so I'm a free man. The judge, with a not-so-happy look on his face, acknowledges the state's appeal request.

I see a bright light coming through the courthouse window. It's decision time again. Do I stop what I'm doing and just run out of the courtroom, then out of City Hall's front doors? Some will look at me funny, but some won't. Some will say, "He's out of here before they change their minds." Others will think it's okay to run if you're free to do so. With that in mind, I go for it. What's a billion dollars if I'm not really living?

Out the courtroom door, down one flight of stairs, then two, and through the large glass and wood revolving doors in front of the building, I run as fast as I can up a marble staircase to ground level. There are people between me and the light, but I focus straight ahead, and it seems like the light is setting like the sun at the end of the street. I run at it, out of my body, over people and cars. The street signs and landmarks disappear, and I have no sense of up or down, so I stop running.

It feels like there are no more steps on the stairs, but I step up or down, anyway. I find myself on my knees, guessing because my legs are bent. I ask God to keep me in my right mind. Then I stand up, guessing because my legs are straight. I rock my head back and pray, looking up, and then I close my eyes only to see more light. It's not black like the dark; I feel like I'm seeing but just looking at nothing. After a minute, I see something in the distance: a vertical line. I can't tell if it's a long line in the distance or a very short one just in front of my face. Another line at the top forms a right angle, then a third; it starts to look like the corner of a room. On my left side, the same thing happens, but there are no walls, floors, or doors.

Something covers the back of me, and I can't touch it. *Am I up against the wall of a padded room or laying on a bed?* With one eye open, I see nothing, so I close my eyes, expecting to see nothing. My mind fills in some of the blanks for me. I ask myself, "Are we on the inside looking out or on the outside looking in?" I don't know which side of the coin would be better. I lay here, motionless, running down memory lane.

I'm outside the gates of my grammar school, built in three sections: blue, white, and yellow. Now, I'm in the passenger side of a Volkswagen Beetle belonging to my first basketball coach, with close friends and teammates in the back. I'm on the campus of my Catholic high school, which looks like a castle. My junior college is up ahead, and I see myself dunking a basketball while waiting for the next pickup game that could have won me an NBA dunk contest. Down the road, I spot the university I didn't graduate from and a girl I had seen before with all kinds of colors in her hair. I later learn she is on the Dean's List; I hope she's okay. Then it's boot camp for me in the United States Air Force.

That's life. I hear it on the news now and think to myself, "Thank God it isn't me falling asleep behind the wheel of a moving car and rolling over four or five times." The reporter says witnesses think he is still alive. The car looks like the one I drive, except I don't have tinted windows. Lucky for him, that car is equipped with roll bars, which keep it from going flat when it's upside down. With all the highway miles I drive, it could easily be me.

The reporter says, "No other cars were involved. On average a person can drive ten to twenty seconds nodding off, depending on the straightness of the road or the alignment of the vehicle. In other news, the police are at the scene of a double murder, details when we return."

At this point, all of what I know is packed together, and some facts have been mixed in with each other, and sometimes I don't know what goes with what. It's kind of good to know I didn't commit this crime or at least found innocent. On the other hand, I don't have a few billion laying around in some offshore bank account, or do I?

I really didn't find the wife in bed with someone else. It had been my version of a "Christmas Carol" future, warning me of what could come if I didn't change my ways.

What about May 21, 2011? That date was supposed to be the end of the world as we know it. What about it? I know I'm as ready as the next person who follows Jesus. I'm sure of that fact. Jesus has prepared a place, taken care of the arrangements, and paid the price for me.

Maybe that's what a few billion dollars is for my heaven. No, I don't think God has so many strings attached. Although, it could be considered as the wealth of the wicked stored up and given to me.

Now we're back to that, trying to convince myself that taking the money would be okay. It would be heaven on earth. No worries over the problem that the lack of money brings. It's all good until someone trips over the cord and pulls it out the wall socket, and I just drop dead in my head like those people in *The Matrix*.

Yes, that's right, stay in the light, which shines all around us by day and by night, hoping the next voice I hear is family. Yes, you may be thinking about it, too. Am I coming out of a coma or dreaming about it? Do I ask for a promotion and get it, or do I steal it? Is it God's favor or curse? So, I stole one last time, I tell myself. Am I forgiven? Yes, as a child of God, but knowing the truth and choosing to do wrong. Well, God forbid that I would think it okay to continue doing wrong.

I have a lot to think about, a few billion to be exact. Even with all the money, would that be real life or just fantasy? I'm thinking it's okay, but at what cost?

The news is on again on the flat screen; I'm in the hospital looking up at the ceiling and I hear the reporter at the scene of an accident.

The reporter, with a sense of urgency and question in her voice, says, "People are going to wonder what went wrong. Did a tractor trailer lose control from equipment malfunction or driver error, or did the truck driver do all he or she could to avoid a passenger car out of control? Whatever you add to the equation, the sum is a pile of twisted metal on fire. To see it from a distance would remind someone of a barn fire big enough to be seen from space. All cars passing are moving slowly so they can see the madness. I have no choice but to watch it as well. Brake lights and headlights for miles accent the highway's hills, curves, and valleys. I'm in heavy nighttime traffic, and not taking for granted that I'm still on my way home. This is not the case for everyone at any given moment. This is My T. Story for Channel 3 News. Back to you, Will."

"In other news…"

I use the remote that operates the bed and sit myself up. A nurse passes my room and doubles back, smiling and jumping up and down like she's jumping rope. Excitement in her greeting, she says, "Welcome back," and calls the doctor.

The nightstand has newspapers on it with a headline that reads: "Home Invasion Leaves Two People Dead, Male Victim Decapitated."

I see the New York skyline out my window, and it looks like a nice day outside. Joy and River have arrived, and they're all smiles. The doctor comes in and gives me a once-over. At the end of the exam, he tells me I might not be able to return to my job because of my injuries. Then the head nurse says, "There are some positions open here at the hospital in the medical supply department. Let me know when you're ready; all you have to do is ask." I think she likes me.

Then, everything changes at once. We watch a plane fly into one of the towers. People are in shock and disbelief as we look from afar. Our eyes are glued to the window, and we can't quite believe what we're seeing, but now we see smoke. Regular programming is interrupted, and it appears on the flat screen. I imagine this is the same type of hypnotic trance we will experience when Jesus cracks the sky on His return. It isn't Jesus. It's the sight of a second plane flying into the other tower in living color and full HD.

All eyes are looking up as the reporter reports. He's asking, "Who's to blame? The pilots, the air traffic controllers, or did the aircraft malfunction? Will the black box tell us anything if they find it? Someone is clearly asleep at the control panel."

Cleo and OM come into the room, both wearing that "I'm not surprised" look on their faces. Our plan depended on the unthinkable happening, and now both damaged buildings are burning. People are jumping out of the windows to avoid an agonizing death—a certain quick death from forty stories up onto the streets below. It seems some have made this choice at the last second, realizing they have no other option or hoping they might survive the fall. What looks like burning debris are actually people falling on fire. From that height, the bodies explode when their mass hits the unyielding concrete.

The reporter says, "If possible, we can have some peace in knowing that most of the people that jumped died from heart attacks or shock before they hit the ground from that height."

While everyone except Cleo, OM, and River looks away from me, I unplug from the machines because they're telling me it's time to go. I give River a note to pass to Joy, kiss her forehead, and hand her my cell phone, telling her she will get a call. I see River reading the note as I walk out the door with Cleo and OM.

CHAPTER 16

The End

I live in two places, bouncing from reality to reality. The details of one will escape memory, so I visit that place in my dreams.

I live a double life. Calamity beyond my control causes the details of both to escape memory like I've fallen and bumped my head.

I'll visit that place in my dreams.

When I dream, I think about my life once I wake up. The fight against double-minded thinking causes actions in both situations to escape the knowing of which is real and the reality of it all.

I visit these places in my dreams. When I see myself there, I wonder what I did to be here.

Moses, David, and Paul were all out of control, even while in the hands of God. I am not saying crime is the way to be closer to God, but because God can. The Great I AM has used these men for His glory and He can use me also; a mighty work with Jesus helping me along the way.

I call River today, letting her know I'm okay. Turns out that having all the money I need in my little world doesn't cure all the ills that come with life. One day, I'll find a safe way back to my River and Joy. I only have a few seconds to talk or leave a message. The Powers That Be check from time to time to see if we—me, myself, and I—really burned as the bodies found beyond DNA recognition.

Next stop, plastic surgery and maybe cutting off my baby toe, so I don't forget to walk with my limp.

MORE PEACE

Acknowledgments

I'm told that acknowledgments are for the people who are instrumental in the process of this product. Me, myself, and I, the editor, the printers, the cover artist, the graphic design person, the team, and the publishing house—all of whose names are in here somewhere. To all of us, I say, *Thank You*, sincerely.

Now, I want to thank the people who make up the foundation of my mindset. You know, where I come from, you dig? I realize I'm not accepting an Academy Award today, but I don't want to miss the chance with never having done so.

I thank God, who is my life. He allowed me to come into this world through the best parents, Brookshire Z., and Brookshire G. III. I want to thank their parents and their parents' parents. My aunts and uncles alike have played a part in the person I have become. Next, I need to mention my wife, the love of my life, LJ, and her parents. This is the village I'm formed in with cousins and friends.

The YMCA is where I learned to swim at age four and where I sat on the Board of Directors at the age of seven or eight years old. I was the go-between for the swim team and the Board of Directors. I gave input on the color of the uniforms and whether we took bag lunches or stopped at

McDonald's on road trips. I am thankful for this experience as it helped to shape me into the upstanding person I have become today.

I thank God for my children: daughter BAB and son TDG. To them, I owe my will to push forward with this life I now live through Christ Jesus. I just can't tell it all.

Special thanks to my brother by blood, Brookshire C., and his whole family. Thank you to my village brothers and their families—you know who you are. Those not mentioned, please charge it to the brown juice and not my heart. There are many forks in the road. We've been making good and bad choices as far back as the first Adam and Eve.

An extra special thank you to editor Sharel Gordon-Love for putting up with me in my first attempt at writing a novel. Extra thanks to Harry Lawson at Enigma Graphics, who crafted the cover from my hand drawing.

I also thank Jessica Tilles of TWA Solutioins & Services for editing and laying out the interior of *Double Dutch*.

Heaven helps us all.

About the Author

Brookshire G. IV is affectionately dubbed "The Bishop" in his home. He is a confirmed pastor and has held an officer's seat at his church for many years. He grew up in Chicago with summers spent in Mississippi.

Brookshire earned an Associate Degree in Business Administration and Education, and a Bachelor's Degree in Theology. He ministers the Word of God in churches, colleges, and workshops. He resides in Pennsylvania, has a son, is married to his childhood sweetheart, and together they have a college-aged daughter.